D1179095

# THE
# DEADLY DYKE

**BRIAN PARVIN**

ROBERT HALE · LONDON

© *Brian Parvin 1979*
*First published in Great Britain 1979*

ISBN 0 7091 7363 6

Robert Hale Limited
Clerkenwell House
Clerkenwell Green
London, EC1R 0HT

For Mary

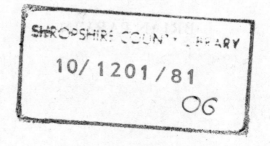
Photoset by
Kelly and Wright
Bradford-on-Avon, Wiltshire
and printed and bound in Great Britain by
Redwood Burn Limited
Trowbridge and Esher

# ONE

There had been neither wind nor rain across the Fens for nearly a month. The land, ploughed ready for early sowing, lay like a curly pile carpet drying to dust under the scorching sun of a freak November. Not a blade of parched grass moved, not a finger of twig stirred on the stiff, lonely trees. Already the dykes linking the fields were dried to spidery parchment and the growth at their sides to the bones of grey skeletons. Above, the sky stretched forever in a smooth blue mass. Below it, the countryside choked on itself and sank deeper into thirst. Another week of this weather and the growers at Cheal End would be rushing lemming-like to drown their sorrows in the night-tide at the estuary eight miles to the east.

But for someone, somewhere, the weather had played a perfect part in a way that could not have been predicted but which, when it presented itself, was to suit the purpose ideally. If murder had to be committed and the body left in a flat landscape without attempting to hide it by digging a grave and unearthing strikingly dark clods, what better than to have four weeks of drought when few people worked or walked the land and the body could be left to quietly, almost reverently decompose? For someone it had certainly been a heaven-sent opportunity and one willingly taken, and had it not been for Charlie Stokes' habit of slipping out of the village at dusk to read a girlie magazine under the bridge at the Cheal Crossing, no one would have discovered the body of

Marcia Tucker until the first rains came.

As it was, Charlie had been given a copy of "Bare" and, eager to discover its thrills, had arrived on that Monday night at the Crossing and slid clumsily down the dyke side to his spot beneath the bridge, just out of sight of any passers-by. It was as he had steadied himself in his slide across the dry grass that he had reached out with his left hand to balance himself and placed it firmly on Marcia's right thigh. And in those few seconds of turning to see and then to recognise who and what he had touched, Charlie Stokes' brow and arm-pits oozed the first water for weeks. . .

## TWO

Murder, as far as Inspector Arthur Mole was concerned, was largely a matter of chance. The chances are, he had once told an academic young Sergeant fresh to the Criminal Investigation Department at Moston, that it would never be committed; thought about, yes, even planned for, but actually done, very rarely. "You see," he had explained from behind his more than usually cluttered desk, "most folk live just this side of the ultimate impulse. Anger and fear well up, go on a wild fling through the mind, wear themselves out, and hop back to bed, if you follow me. And what seemed like a blue-black hell an hour ago, ends up as harmless abuse. It's the pattern." Not that on occasions the impulse did not get the upper hand — and then, bang, there was the body and there, poised over it bloody and bewildered, a killer.

But such a person had simply killed, which, in his

opinion, was quite different from murdering. "Your killer acts out the impulse. Your murderer experiences the impulse, takes it in hand and masters it, then shapes it into carefully planned elimination. And that type is the worst because he's weighed up the chances of successfully accomplishing the act and come to the conclusion that he can risk it and beat the odds of being found out. And for all you know, he probably will."

Murder and killings, however, were far from everyday happenings in that part of Fenland—and for two reasons, Mole believed. Firstly, a hard working rural atmosphere where people were far more concerned with the life of their crops than with the death of an enemy; and second, a small, scattered population. Moston, the largest town in the county, although far from rating as a city, still had a population of under fifty thousand. There was another equally significant reason to have emerged in recent years: the young bloods did not usually stay in the area. Much of the potentially vicious element drifted away to the industrial centres, leaving Inspector Mole and his team with theft, seasonal traffic problems and the occasional Saturday night brawl as the most they were called upon to handle.

For Mole, it was an acceptable state of affairs. He had no feverish ambition to play the big policeman in some neon-saturated city, where the best to be hoped for was a small circle of makeshift friends and a Saturday afternoon blow of fresh air, always assuming you were lucky enough to find the time and not too worn out to drive for half a day to find it. In Moston, he enjoyed respect, knew enough people personally to be hailed as "Arthur" in the streets, was as familiar with the town and the surrounding villages as he was with his own garden, and a part of a police team that was just large enough to recognise rank without letting position degenerate into petty hates or boot-licking worship.

Moston, the Force, the setting, the people and the mood of the Fenland suited him. All he had ever wished for was, that at forty-seven years of age, he had given some thought earlier in life to the prospects of marriage. But the bachelor life in the small but untidy cottage at Bird Dyke was not all snatched meals and lonely week-ends. There was his glasshouse and the chrysanthemums, occasional visits from friends — and time to think. Even so, perhaps the closeness of a woman might have made a difference. . .

Whatever closeness Marcia Tucker had enjoyed, it had not done her much good, thought Mole, as he stared at the set of photographs spread across his desk. He picked up the portrait shot of her — an attractive, clean featured woman in her late twenties; blonde, hazel-eyed, with a gentle, well-shaped mouth that would have showed small, cared-for teeth when she smiled. He turned to the shots taken of the body at the Cheal Crossing. They were not gruesome; there was nothing sadistic or brutal about her death, only the fact that the body had lain for three days in the sun and the face and exposed areas of flesh become burned and started to decompose added any horror to what might otherwise have been no more than a shot of a woman asleep in the grass. True, the body was partly clothed — she or the killer had removed either a skirt or slacks and the lower half of her underwear — but the actual killing seemed to him to have been a straightforward job, executed with great care and considerable premeditation; one quick but highly effective stab with, so the medical report said, a "thin bladed knife, the type that might be found in any kitchen." There were no signs of a struggle having taken place and the body had not been dumped at the spot. From the position of the body and the quantity of congealed blood found on the earth and grass, it seemed that Marcia had met a lover at the Crossing and layed down with him in the seclusion of the bridge's shadow—just as she may have done on many previous occasions. With the same man, he wondered, or had Marcia Tucker been a free-wheeling date at Cheal End?

"We know a fair bit about her, sir," said Sergeant Fisher, seating himself opposite Mole and opening the brown foolscap file. "She was a local girl, born at Cheal Gate, the next village. One of a family of four—two brothers, both in Canada, and a sister living in London. Parents died about five years ago. She was well educated—won a scholarship to Moston High—and seemed all set into a career as a librarian, then she married John Tucker and they ran a small farm at Cheal End. A mixed bag, some growing, a few pigs, egg production, that sort of thing. Seems they scraped together a living somehow, but it was all a bit hand-to-mouth and a lot of hard work. There were no children. John Tucker died about a year ago. He'd been ill for sometime and a sudden heart attack finished him. She continued the farm with hired casual labour and the help of some of the locals. But there was a deal of bad feeling about because Tucker's brother, Alan, who owns the neighbouring farm Blackstock, flatly refused to give Marcia any assistance. Local talk is that he thought Marcia should have added her spread to his, but she refused to sell, so he refused to help her—and never the two did meet, so to speak. Apparently, they had an almighty row about it in the local pub one night just after Tucker's death, and that was that."

"Did she make a go of the place?" asked Mole.

"Not really, sir. She managed right enough for a month or so, with the first flush of sympathy, you might say, and there didn't seem to be any shortage of helpers. Word soon got around the drifters that there was easy work to be had at Tucker's—with only a woman to give

9

the orders—but they exploited the situation, filched from her left, right and centre, until she was forced to give them up. A few of the locals continued to help, but many of them sided with Alan Tucker and felt she should sell the place to him. So, after six months or so, the place was running down fast and she must have been living on whatever capital her husband left."

"Much?"

"About two-thousand, plus the farm contracts to supply, which weren't many and soon dried up."

"So?"

"So she took to living it up a bit, sir. Nights out in Moston, too much drink by the sound of things, trips to the cities on spending sprees—that sort of thing."

"Men?"

"Well, yes and no sir. She had a reputation for being a bit easy—and everyone seems to have known about it, but no one locally ever saw her doing any 'entertaining' at the farm. Of course, she could have been carrying on during the trips out, but it doesn't sound as if she was making it that obvious."

"But she did have someone close to her, Sergeant?"

"Must have, sir. But you'd be hard pushed to pin him down."

"No one at Cheal End, you mean?"

"Well, sir, you know these Fen villages as well as I do—you can't sneeze without a dozen handkerchiefs hanging under your nose, and it'd soon have been out if she'd had a man in Cheal itself. No, there wasn't anyone locally—at least, not in my opinion. I think you've got to look further afield, sir, perhaps even to the cities."

"Maybe, Sergeant, maybe. Who gets the farm now?"

"Talk is that she'll have left it to one of her brothers. She always said she would, though heaven knows what either of them'll do with it, being in Canada. Solicitors are Robins and Tuttle, by the way."

"What about the house? Have you been in?"

"No one's touched it, sir. I've had it secured and there's a man out there now. You can look it over when you're ready."

"Good," said Mole, getting to his feet. "Then that's where we'll begin, Sergeant. Meanwhile, put someone on to making a few inquiries round the pubs in Moston. Let's see just how well-known our Mrs Tucker was."

"Yes, sir."

"And we'll drop off at the Crossing on our way to the farm. I'd like a closer look at that dyke side."

Mole reached for his hat and jacket. "In a case of elimination, Sergeant, it pays to give everything more than a second glance."

So it was "murder", thought Fisher, as he followed Mole out of the office. He sighed. Then it was going to be a long job. There'd be endless questioning, and then more questions, and the Inspector would start to pace about like a lost dog in a fairground. Oh, well. . .

"Any sign of rain, Sergeant?" asked Mole, as they reached the already waiting car in the street.

"Not a hope, sir," groaned Fisher. "It's another grand day for some, I suppose," he added ruefully.

THREE

The Fenland landscape isn't really a landscape at all, mused Mole, as the car left the last of the houses in better-class Moston and headed into the open country-side; it's a skyscape sitting on flat ground. But it never failed to fascinate him. How was it, he wondered, that men could live and work so cheerfully in such a bleak setting, where the shape of a single tree stood out on the horizon like some leftover on an otherwise clean dinner plate; where the wind whirled and turned in great gasps of asthmatic breathing; where there were no hedgerows and crops grew sheer to the roadside, and every inch of land seemed to have been set to work as though on the production line of some giant agricultural factory; and where, most of all, there were never any surprises round the next bend in the road? You could always see exactly where you'd come from and where you were going to. It was all a bit like living at the centre of time — there was yesterday, here was today, and there coming up ahead, was tomorrow.

Yesterday, or to be more precise, three days ago. . . What he would have given to be able to look back to that Friday when Marcia Tucker kept her date at the Cheal Crossing. Had she come eagerly, even lovingly to the rendezvous, or had it been a meeting she would have preferred to pass over? Had it been a hurried arrangement, or one she had known of for some time; was it a regular meeting place? Perhaps Charlie Stokes could answer that. But why had she gone to the Crossing? If the assignation was purely one of meet, make love, kiss goodbye, then why not the farm? Fear of being seen? Perhaps. Then why so close to the village — and why not, if Sergeant Fisher's information was correct and she was not in the habit of entertaining locally, have insisted on a meeting at "his" place, whoever "he" was? And who was "he"? Someone she knew well, was in love with perhaps, or had she tossed care to the Fenland winds and embarked on a string of lovers?

Or had the whole arrangement been skilfully manoeuvred by "him" under the cover of the need for an urgent meeting with the sole intention of making quite certain that Marcia Tucker was never seen alive again? In which case, she had got in someone's way; she had become a threat of such magnitude that she had to be silenced permanently. But why? Wife trouble for "him", perhaps. Supposing, thought Mole, as he eased back into the soft leather of the car's back seat, supposing she had taken up with some married man. He could be anywhere, in Cheal End, in Moston, or any one of a hundred villages in the county. And supposing "he" had suspected that his wife knew of the affair and, in fear of the consequences, decided to put an end to both it and Marcia. Or suppose the wife had perhaps confronted "him" with the fact that she knew what was going on — and, in so many words, said: her or me, or else. Or else what? Ruin for a prominent man, someone respected and looked up to by the community? There was enough image building based on respectability round here, thought Mole, for a man to risk even murder for the sake of his name.

Then what about blackmail? Had Marcia Tucker been threatening "him" with exposure unless he paid up — she needed the money bad enough by the sound of it. Had "he" reached the end of the payment line? A possibility. But on second thoughts, no. No? But why no? He did not know, except that whoever had murdered Marcia Tucker had controlled the impulse to kill to a point where it had become planned elimination, and that took time and care. It did not spring from sudden anger or final desperation. It festered into a cold, calculated blueprint for death . . .

"What are we missing in the way of clothing, Sergeant?" said Mole abruptly, jerking out of his reverie as the car took a sharp turn off the main road and pulling himself into a more Inspector-like position.

"Well, it's hard to say, sir," said Fisher, half-turning from the front seat towards Mole. "We know what she was wearing above the belt — green blouse and pink bra—but the rest was missing. It's my guess a fairly lightweight skirt in this weather—perhaps cotton or something like that—a pair of panties, perhaps tights, and shoes.''

"No handbag?"

"Could be, sir, but that would have been taken by the killer, I suppose, along with the rest.''

"Why take them?''

"I don't honestly know, sir. Unless they gave something away or could have been associated with the killer, but it seems unlikely. Of course, they could have been a sort of kinky prize.'' Fisher strained his eyes round still further for a reaction on Mole's face. "You know, sir. . .''

"No, Sergeant, I don't think so.''

"Well—,'' began Fisher, facing the open road again.

"You can rest assured,'' said Mole sharply, "that this wasn't a sex killing. It was a carefully planned murder by someone who Marcia Tucker thought enough of to meet in the middle of the afternoon for what we assume to be the purpose of making love. You saw the Pathologist's estimated time of death?''

"Yes, sir. Between three and six on Friday, as near as he could say, bearing in mind that it was yesterday before the body was found.''

"It's getting dusk by five, even on a good day,'' said Mole. "So my guess is that they met sometime between three and four. She was dead by five-thirty for certain.''

"That seems reasonable, sir. But why at the Crossing, that's what beats me. I'd have thought it'd have been more comfortable. . .''

"We'll stop this side of the bridge and walk up to it,'' interrupted Mole.

"Yes, sir.''

The bridge at Cheal Crossing is appropriately named, for the only way of reaching Cheal End from the direction of Moston is by crossing the old stone structure at this point. Miss it, and the visitor is forced to continue for another two miles along the dyke side to the turning to Fosbrick, which then winds its way for a further three miles before entering Cheal End by the back door. The village, a collection of stone cottages, a church, a pub (the Five Cats) two shops and a ramshackle garage operated on a part-time basis by a local farmer, can be seen quite clearly from the bridge, its shape sprawled across the land like the humped back of some sleeping animal. Surrounding it, is an expanse of flat, but cultivated land that stretches grey, brown and sometimes green to the distant horizon, broken here and there by the jagged line of a pine tree wind-break or the sharp geometry of a farm house, barn or machine shed. For the rest, it is rich earth which through the seasons, swells its acres to crops of sugar-beet, cauliflowers and potatoes, and in some years, smears of dazzling daffodils and tulips in mile-long regimented bloom.

Cheal End is isolated and far removed from anything connected with modern civilisation, and yet by Fenland standards, it is thought of as prosperous and thriving. Good men farm good land in Cheal End, and only a few, like the Tuckers, come to a grievous end. Others live, breed, prosper and grow old quietly, reflecting on the bumper crops and high market prices of past years and cherishing their good fortune at having been born where they were.

And for this reason as much as any other, thought Mole, as he and Fisher walked along the dykeside in the direction of the bridge, the people of Cheal End preserve an independence and honesty among themselves which would be difficult to disturb. Why, he wondered, had they sided with Alan Tucker in his belief that Marcia should sell out to him? The commonsense of sound economics among a community who knew only too well the disasters that could lurk behind any season's growing; or was it something deeper, something she had brought about herself during those first six months following her husband's death? Had Marcia Tucker been forced to turn her back on Cheal End and her friends, or had they turned their back on her because of the way of life she had chosen?

"If it doesn't rain soon, this place'll be a dust bowl," said Fisher, mopping his brow with a large handkerchief. "It's like the bloody tropics! Not a breath is there, sir?"

Mole stopped and scuffed his right toe cap in the grass. "Lifeless," he said, removing his hat and mopping his own brow. "Yet underneath, there's a mass of life waiting to get started. All it needs is the push of some rain."

"Yes, sir," said Fisher, still mopping.

"That's what must have happened to Marcia Tucker. Something pushed her—only the other way. Into death."

Fisher put away his handkerchief. "Do you honestly think it was a local job, sir? You know, done by somebody over there"—he pointed towards the village—"or within a mile or so, or perhaps even Moston? Couldn't it just as easily have been one of the casual workers—sort of getting his own back for being laid off or not getting what he hoped for?"

"There's nothing to prove you wrong at the moment, Sergeant," said Mole. "Nothing at all. But I don't somehow see Marcia Tucker walking here to meet some fly-by-night casual worker."

"Young widows get to doing strange things, sir."

"Not young widows of Marcia Tucker's type—at least, not as I see it. Still, you could be right. Come on, let's take a look at the spot. If only it could talk, eh Sergeant!"

"Probably just ask for a drink, sir!"

Mole laughed. "You're right, Sergeant, it probably

would!"

They quickened their pace down the narrow road, Mole letting his gaze flick over the parched growth of the dykeside like a dragon-fly on the wing, Fisher raising a hand to shield his eyes from the sun's glare as he scanned the fields around Cheal End. "There's the Tucker place," he said, pointing to a small bungalow surrounded by a collection of outbuildings on the edge of the village.

"She didn't have far to walk," said Mole.

"Somebody must've seen her, sir. You can't walk far in this country without being spotted a mile off."

"Perhaps somebody did. Better get onto that. Put out a general call then a house-to-house check in the village."

"Yes, sir."

The bridge is just wide enough to take a lorry. Its low parapets are chipped and grazed where drivers in a hurry have misjudged the swing from the road and cursed as their vehicle's tail-end made contact with the ancient stone. Below it, the dry dyke bed lay partly in shadow from the bridge's side, then stretched away in a straight line as far as the eye could see. The body had lain to the right of the bridge, three-quarters of the way down the smooth, sloping side. All that could be seen now of the position was an area of flattened growth and a dark patch of dried blood from which thinner streaks spread like spiky fingers over and through the grass stalks to the bottom of the dyke.

Mole stood staring at the spot for a full minute before easing himself down the slope and into the shadow. He turned to look underneath the bridge, into a semi-darkness that blinded him for a moment; then he walked into it. In spite of the weather, there was a damp, musty smell here and his shoes left their imprints on spongier ground. There was no water, but neither was the mud baked dry as elsewhere. He crouched, waited for his eyesight to adjust to the half light, and peered at the surface beneath him. There were certainly no marks to indicate a recent presence, nothing so fortuitous as a set of footprints or a hand mark, but there was something that caught his eye. He reached out to the tiny, shining object and picked it up. A thimble.

"Anything of interest, sir?" called Fisher from the road.

"I'm not sure," said Mole, reappearing from beneath the bridge and standing upright again in the dyke. "Unless you call a thimble interesting."

Mole scrambled back to the roadside and lay the find in the palm of his hand. "One thing's for sure, it hasn't been there more than a few days. It's too clean and it wasn't embedded in the mud."

"Marcia Tucker's?" asked Fisher.

"Perhaps. Or it could be a child's."

"Or dropped by a bird. Magpies do that sort of thing you know, sir."

"Or perhaps the murderer's?"

"Seems a bit unlikely, sir. How many men go around with a thimble in their pocket?"

"Not many," agreed Mole. "But somebody did — and lost it." He pocketed the object and turned his gaze in the direction of the village. "Get the car down here, Sergeant, and we'll take a look at the farm."

# FOUR

Tucker's Farm, as it was known locally, had once been no more than a wooden shack and outbuildings, without sanitation, running water or mains electricity.

18

But by the time John Tucker had taken over ownership, the shack had been replaced by a two-bedroom bungalow, complete with kitchen-cum-dining area, and a lounge; a flush toilet had replaced the bucket in the shed and electricity had brought some of the comforts of modern living. It was into this setting that Tucker had brought his young bride, intent, as he had told her, on building the place up until they had a thriving livelihood from its fifty acres. Within a year, they had constructed a small piggery, converted one of the two barns into a bulb-sorting shed and replaced some of the tumbled-down outbuildings with newer and more spacious designs. In the following year, they concentrated on more efficient management and sowing of the acreage and, with as few hired hands as possible and doing most of the work themselves from dawn until dusk, succeeded in seeing a small return for their efforts.

Locally, they were admired for their industry and determination to make the venture a paying proposition. It took the spirit of youth to work the land in times of frustrating economic shifts and uncertainty in the market place, but given courage and conviction, said those older, wiser and a deal more battered than the Tuckers, a living could be made. No doubt this would have been the case had John Tucker not taken ill and for almost the whole of one season been confined to his bed. Marcia, however, had carried on, stretching the hours of each day to include the work of the farm and tending to the needs of her husband. Some good contracts were lost, but they would return or be replaced once John was fit again — that, at least had been her hope.

John's recovery, however, had been slow and, for the doctors concerned with his case, baffling in its spasms of sudden buoyancy that turned just as unexpectedly to periods of intense depression and exhaustion. Nevertheless, by the start of the following year he was free of the sick bed and regular hospital visits and making, as he described it, lazy but steady progress. He was unable to tackle the more strenuous tasks around the farm, but with care and patience he was able to supervise the help they had and ensure that it was put to the best use. He busied himself with the accounting, with the prospects for the season to come and in devising ways and means of making improvements. He even worked out a new crop rotation scheme — thought up in the small hours when sleep seemed as distant as the moon he watched from the bedroom window.

What concerned him more than the day-to-day round of jobs, however, and which did nothing to encourage the rest and worry-free weeks the doctors had prescribed for complete recovery, was Marcia's state of health. She claimed cheerfully enough that the hard work and the long days did not trouble her, that she was doing it all for them and that "it would not always be dark at six." Then, with a smile and a hug for John, she would set out for the fields as though relishing the challenge, determined that a setback of ill-health should not be allowed to ruin their future. But as the weeks passed and John's health still confined him to menial tasks, he noticed a weariness clouding her face. The cheeriness disappeared, the hugs became less meaningful and the determination lapsed into a quiet resignation of meeting each day and each chore as it came. Her tiredness intensified and with it came an irritability that made her snap at the slightest inconvenience. Her interest in the home was drowned in a tide of too much outdoor work and not enough time for either. As each day ended, so she turned to see so little accomplished. Nothing ever seemed to get finished. The end of one job, only half completed in some cases, spelt the beginning of another and that in turn to yet another, until the tasks became a heap of confusion, frustration and eventually indecision.

By now John had decided on his own course of action and, turning medical advice aside, he set about a normal day's work. At first, Marcia had objected violently, calling him a fool and even threatening on one occasion to leave him, but as she saw his determination to pull his weight again, so she had given in—partly in desperation, partly in thankfulness for another pair of hands. And so they had continued for another two years, with John's health as temperamental as the March winds and both their lives sealed, it seemed, in the clods of dark earth they ploughed.

Two days after John Tucker was buried in the small churchyard at Cheal End, Marcia had stood alone in the barn they had built and resolved that somehow she would carry on. In a strange, hypnotic way, his death had come as no sudden shock. She had found it difficult to cry; the tears were there but walled up in the harshness of the life they had led and the cruelty of their fate, in the effort that had been expended and the dreams they had worked for but known were beyond them.

He had died peacefully. Marcia had returned from the fields to find him asleep, as she thought, in his chair, but when she had bent to give him a hug and ask if he would like a warm drink, he had slumped across her arms, heavy, cold and dead. For a moment, she had held him close, her grip tightening on his already lifeless body. And all she had been able to say was, "Oh, John."

In the weeks that followed, her resolve to continue the work at Tucker's Farm rose and fell with the regularity of day to night. She would be cheerful at an offer of help, then disillusioned and bitter at some hired hand's attempts to swindle her; market prices would hold, she would make a good sale and her spirits would rise only to be choked again by a machine breakdown, a dead piglet, a shoddy crop. If only there had been someone close to her, as close as John had been. If only she had been able to bear him a child. . . .

## FIVE

"You can tell there's never been any kids around this place," said Fisher as he and Mole walked into the lounge at Tucker's Farm. "Funny, but houses without kids are always the same — sort of empty and lost."

Mole sensed the emptiness. In spite of the furniture, most of it second-hand and threadbare, the room had neither character nor colour. Everything was in its place, neat and tidy, but with an order that left Mole feeling that nothing had ever been used as it should. The chairs were old and sagging, the settee collapsed at one end, and the table scratched in places and stained, but these were the marks of weariness, not those made in the pleasure of use. John Tucker had crumpled into his chair at night, tired, weary and bewildered. He had not sat in it to relax with a newspaper or book or to watch television; there had been no comfort among the cushions, only somewhere to ease his body and let it subside into a state of half-sleeping limbo.

The kitchen and bedrooms were much the same, there but not lived in — walls without pictures or prints, encompassing items of purely functional furniture.

Mole went back to the lounge. In one corner was a bureau, opened, with a small pile of letters on the desk. He skimmed through them — the usual circulars, two football coupons, a letter with a London postmark, some bills, a bank statement, and lastly an unopened envelope bearing the name and address of a Moston firm of solicitors, Robins & Tuttle, 5 Low Walk, Moston. He tidied the pile, replaced it on the desk and joined Fisher in the kitchen.

"Doesn't look as if she'd been eating too well," said Fisher opening and closing cupboard doors. "There's hardly enough here to keep a mouse alive."

"Seen a sewing box or bag on your travels?" asked Mole tightening a dripping tap at the sink.

"No, can't say I have, sir. Any particular reason?"

"I just thought we might find a home for the thimble," said Mole.

"I'll take another look, sir. We could have missed it. But I don't reckon she'd have had much time for sewing—a quick needle and thread job would've had to do."

Mole walked through the lounge again and along the short corridor that led to the bedrooms. The first, a small room with a single bed and bedside cabinet, had never been used, he guessed. It would have been thought of as the spare, or perhaps been planned as a nursery. The second had been the Tucker's room. Here was a double-bed, two bedside cabinets, a dressing-table and a large oak wardrobe, forty years old if it was a day. He opened its double-doors.

For the first time since entering the greyness of the house, with its tired rooms and functional arrange-ment, colour and character hit him full in the face. Here were clothes—skirts, dresses, coats, slacks, knitwear—in as bright an array of colours as any boutique would display. Below the racks of Marcia Tucker's fashionable indulgences were what seemed to Mole to be enough pairs of shoes to compete with any Moston stockist. Still unopened packs of tights filled one corner, and lining the back of the wardrobe were handbags of every conceivable shape, size and colour in sufficient quantity to have allowed her to carry a different style every day of the week.

Snuggled into the opposite corner was a small decoupage decorated wooden casket. Mole lifted it out and was surprised to find the lid unlocked. Inside, was a jumbled mass of jewellery—ear-rings, pendants, brooches, bangles, strings of beads and pearls, rings, some of no greater value than could have been bought in any Woolworths, but others, such as the ring he held in his fingers, of considerable beauty and, he guessed, worth.

"Better take charge of this lot, Sergeant," said Mole as Fisher joined him in the room. "And get a value on it." He handed over the casket.

"Ye gods!" gasped Fisher, eyeing the wardrobe's contents. "So that's where the money went!"

"Some of it, certainly," said Mole. He closed the doors and moved to the dressing-table. Here was everything he would have expected to find—make-up, hair-brushes, a collection of perfumes, a box of tissues, one screwed to a ball and stained with orange lipstick, and a tortoise-shell comb. He picked it up. Clinging to its teeth were strands of black hair.

"She was a blonde, wasn't she?"

"Natural, sir," said Fisher.

"Then she'd had a visitor. Here." He handed the comb to Fisher. "Better keep an eye on that as well. See what the Lab boys come up with."

He was about to turn away from the table and go back to the lounge when he noticed a neatly folded slip of paper placed beneath a ceramic posy of flowers. It was a doctor's prescription made out to Mrs M. Tucker on a form headed Dr J.S. Hill, The Barn, Cheal End. As he expected, the prescription details were beyond his fathoming, but it was dated August, four months ago.

"I didn't know the village had its own doctor," said Mole.

"She's new, sir. A lady doctor, Jeanne Hill, just come down from Yorkshire. She covers Cheal End and one or two of the neighbouring villages."

"Alright," said Mole, placing the form between the folds of his wallet, "that's it Sergeant. Now, where's Alan Tucker's place — what's it called?"

"Blackstock, sir, and it's just across the fields," said Fisher, following Mole through the lounge, into the kitchen and out through the back door. "The two farms adjoin each other, which is why he was so keen to get his hands on it, I suppose. Would have given him a big spread."

Mole adjusted his hat against the sunlight. "No sign of that sewing bag?"

"No, sir," said Fisher. "I found a card of needles and some cotton — oh, and two knitting needles — but no sewing bag or box."

Mole shrugged.

"Want to take a look round the outbuildings, sir?"

Mole turned his gaze across the yard to the clutter of buildings at the far end. Again, he was struck by the same weary orderliness he had sensed indoors. The yard was not untidy, the buildings neither ramshackle nor in need of major repairs, but everywhere — in the timber, the doors, the few empty crates, the tackle, tractor and hand tools scattered about — there was an air of resignation, perhaps of defeat, as though each item had finally given up, glad to be free of its responsibilities. For a second, Mole sensed a chill at the back of his neck. This isn't a farm, he thought, it's a cemetery.

"No, I don't think so," he said. "Who's taking care of the stock? You mentioned pigs and poultry."

"Yes, sir, the piggery's round there, at the back of the barn. One of Alan Tucker's men is looking to them till things are sorted out. Anyway, there's only two. She sold the others, and the poultry."

"Fair enough," said Mole, "but don't let him go wandering about all over the place."

"Just so, sir. I'm keeping a round-the-clock watch on

the farm for another day or so with our men from Moston. Then Lumby—he's the local man—will take over."

"Very good," said Mole, walking back to the car.

As they turned left out of the gate and headed towards Blackstock, Mole looked back at the bungalow. It might, he thought, have been a headstone above a grey, silent grave: Here lies hope, taken from us suddenly. . .


# SIX

By contrast with Tucker's Farm, Blackstock was all hustle, bustle, noise and movement. As the car eased its way through the open paddock-style gates and into the scrubbed yard, Mole sensed the urgency of purpose as he watched half a dozen workers hurrying about their separate jobs. Two tractors coughed into life and swung casually across the car's path, the drivers giving a wide wave as they passed. From the large open-side barns came the sound of piped music beating out a popular rhythm in time to the female labour's lightning flash of hands as they sifted through an eternity of bulbs, placing some here, some there, tossing others into pallets at their sides. To Mole's left, three men hand-loaded a wagon with boxes, throwing them chain pattern from the first, to the second and finally to the third man perched high on the wooden mountain.

The car stopped. A thick-set black and white collie dog wandered inquisitively out of its domain among a heap of sacks, barked a welcome and was joined in a scurry of bristling fur from behind the barn by a slimmer version that pranced and danced round the car wheels. If Tucker's Farm had been a cemetery, this was a cabaret, thought Mole.

"Shall we pull over to the house, sir?" said Fisher, tapping the Constable driver on the shoulder and indicating a rambling two-storey house to their right.

"It might be easier," said Mole, winding up the back window and shutting out the noise.

"Over there," instructed Fisher.

The car swished over a short gravel drive to the lattice porch at the front door, stopped, and Mole got out. He turned to watch the two tractors trundling their way down the narrow road, and then to the sleek collie standing, front paws on the drive, back legs on the yard, undecided as to whether Mole was friend or foe. From inside the bulb barn, a woman whistled provocatively at him. That, he thought, hadn't happened to him in years. . .

"You catch us at a busy time of day, Inspector," said a voice behind him. "It is Inspector Mole, I presume? I'm Alan Tucker."

Mole turned. He had spent the few minutes drive from Tucker's Farm to Blackstock considering what type of a man he should expect in Alan Tucker: hefty, hard working, with a weather-tooled face and a fussy wife who scuttled about the farmhouse kitchen like an over maternal hen; or perhaps a slow talking, lumbering man, steeped in Fenland traditions, with a permanent scowl and eyes that probed deep as though assessing a man's face as a potential seed bed. Or perhaps none of these. Perhaps he would be just ordinary in shirt sleeves and slacks, with a tanned, cheerful glow and a wife to match.

Mole had been hopelessly wrong. Alan Tucker was immediately out of place and out of time in the Fens. He was tall, nearing six-feet, mid-forties, slim, and almost exotically casual in olive green silk shirt, fawn flannels and soft suede shoes. He stood easily, hands in pockets, but erect, his unusually clear blue eyes looking down on Mole from beneath a page-boy setting of thick black hair topping a lean likable face. There were no obviously attractive features about him, just a level measure of handsome proportions. He'd have made it in films, thought Mole, as he took the long hand offered him.

"Good afternoon, Mr Tucker," said Mole. "Yes, I'm Inspector Mole, and this is Sergeant Fisher. Would it be convenient to have a word with you, sir?"

"Certainly, Inspector," said Tucker, ushering Mole and Fisher through the porch, the open front door and into a cool, shadowed room to their right. "I thought my study," he said closing the door. "It's cool here through the afternoon. Odd, isn't it, that we should be so intent on seeking the shade in this country?"

"Quite a change of climate," smiled Mole, "but a talking point."

"Indeed, yes." Tucker walked to the windows and half-closed them. "Shut out the noise. Now, Inspector, Sergeant, what can I offer you — nothing too strong, I imagine, but would an iced drink go down well, or will it be coffee or tea? A Scotch if you prefer it, of course."

"Thank you, sir, the iced drinks would be admirable," said Mole, placing his hat on the desk in the window.

"Good, then I'll organise that. My wife will be down in a moment. You did want to see my wife as well, I take it?"

"If it's convenient, sir, it would be useful."

"No problem. Excuse me a moment."

"Talk about chalk and cheese," said Fisher when Tucker had left the room, closing the door behind him. "How the other half lives, eh sir?"

Mole grinned. "This half of the family seems to have made it, I agree."

He glanced round the room. For a study, it was more like an arrangement of antiques and furniture he had once seen designed by a Harrods' window-dresser. Taking up almost the entire length of one wall was a bookcase and shelving for objets d'art; thick gold-tooled volumes covering subjects as diverse as the classics to sumptuous coffee table editions of guides to the gardens and stately homes of Britain, with, at one end, case-bound editions of farming publications and journals, and placed strategically through them in carefully balanced spacing, items of pottery, snuff boxes and exquisite figurines in lace-like detail that should, thought Mole, have carried DO NOT TOUCH notices.

The room's carpet was thick wall-to-wall shades of cream and soft brown; the walls panelled, the furniture discreet and inoffensive, not too heavy for the area so that you felt chained to carved legs and velvet cushions, but not that lightweight or spindly that it floated out of sight. Four excellent Turner reproductions were hung to the best advantage of available light, and on the clear highly polished desk top stood a genuine Victorian oil lamp. Mole doubted if Alan Tucker ever worked in here — the desk drawers, he was willing to wager, were empty — but as a public relations parlour, it took some beating.

"As you will have gathered, Inspector, I was expecting you," said Tucker as he came back to the room, this time carrying a tray of two tall glasses of orange drink in which ice cubes clinked invitingly. He placed the tray on the desk. "Help yourselves." He waited until Mole and the Sergeant had sampled their drinks, then continued, "I hadn't known precisely when, of course, but I guessed it would be soon. A terrible affair, Inspector. Terrible."

Mole lifted the glass to his lips again and stared over its rim at Tucker. Terrible it was for some, terrible it may be to others but less so — but terrible for Alan Tucker? No, thought, Mole, as he scanned Tucker's face. There was nothing here to suggest that he personally had suffered any pain at the murder of his sister-in-law.

"Naturally," Tucker was saying with a wave to the window, "I appreciate that I must be a suspect, nevertheless . . ."

"Why's that, sir?" said Mole, lowering his glass and turning it between cupped hands. "It's early days yet," he added softly.

Tucker stared directly into Mole's eyes. "Well, I just assumed that you would have heard of the — how shall I put it — the cross purposes at which Marcia and I found ourselves after my brother's death."

"Yes, sir, we have heard some talk along those lines."

"Then there's no need for me to spell it out. But look" — he walked behind the desk and stood, finger-tips spread across it to take his weight, and shoved head and shoulders forward into Mole's gaze — "let's take it from the top." He paused, eased back and for the first time since their meeting, let his face relax. He has lines, Mole noticed, grey lines.

"Blackstock was founded by my Father at the turn of the century. It wasn't much in those days, Inspector, just a stretch of wild land with the wind to keep you company. But Amos Tucker was no fool, and in less than five years he had the foundations of a farm. Nothing to set the world alight, but something he could shape." Tucker paused again. Now his fingers rested lightly on the desk top. "It's the shaping of things that counts, Inspector. It's all very well a man having brawn and breath, but it's brain that finally takes the profit from the earth. My Father had brain. He could see even in those days that, agreed, ploughing, sowing, reaping called for strength, but it was *how* you sowed that dictated *what* you reaped, and *where* you ploughed that brought the right crop at the right time for the right market. And things haven't changed. Spare an acre of land the thought and consideration of planning, and you'll reap an acre of loss." He sat down in the chair at the desk. "Please, do have a seat."

"That's alright, sir," said Mole, "we're used to our feet. Carry on."

"Well, the farm prospered. Two sons were born, myself and John, and by the time we were at our first school you could say that Blackstock was established and my Father become—I was going to say a gentleman farmer, but that's not so in the strict sense of the image. Let's say he was able to take things easier and enjoy the fruits of his effort—and, more important, plan for the farm's future. You follow me?"

"I think so, sir," said Mole.

"Not to bore you with the technicalities, Inspector, but Blackstock had become big, really big, in the bulb world, with some first-rate contacts and associations in Holland and a booming market here. By standards at that time, we were in the top class. And that's when the trouble began."

"Trouble, sir?" said Mole, finishing his drink and returning the glass to the tray. "What sort of trouble?"

"Oh, nothing criminal," said Tucker, leaning back in the chair, his arms loose at his sides. "The sort of trouble you get when a Father discovers that he has two sons of totally opposite outlooks, interests, characteristics— and capabilities. A smouldering trouble, Inspector, of doubts and misgivings." He waited, half smiled and placed his hands, palms down, on the desk. "John and I were complete opposites. John was slow at school, I was quick. John missed a scholarship, I got it. John came to the farm at fifteen, I went on to University. John made Corporal during National Service, I was commissioned. John stayed in the Fens, I travelled. And when it came to

31

my Father making a decision about the future, John got a gift of fifty acres to make of what he could, and I got Blackstock."

"A bit drastic," said Mole.

Tucker came to his feet. "You may think so, Inspector, but the fact is that my Father thought John to be worth no more than fifty acres — and as things have turned out, it seems he was right."

## SEVEN

Tucker stared down at the empty desk top as though in quiet shame at having been forced to make the admission. His hands came slowly back to his lap and he sighed heavily.

"You mean to say your brother was an incompetent farmer?" asked Mole.

"I wouldn't say incompetent," said Tucker, looking up again. "It was more a question of indecision. The farm had no shape, Inspector. One minute he was heavily into pigs, the next it was all egg production, then he'd switch to bulbs. No pattern, you see, no shape."

"Didn't he feel some resentment at being given the fifty acres while you have Blackstock?"

"I think he did — not that he showed it. We were on reasonably good terms."

"And his wife — what did she feel?"

Tucker's head sat firmly on his shoulders now and his eyes narrowed slightly. "She didn't discuss the matter a great deal, not with me, anyway. It was after John's death that her feelings came to the surface. She was angry, bitter. I think she may have felt cheated. Then, when I approached her about merging the farm with Blackstock, she told me to forget it — forever. She said I'd got enough and that even if it killed her" — he looked quickly, self-consciously at Mole at the use of the phrase — "she'd keep the place going. I offered her a good price, more than it is worth, in fact, but she wouldn't listen. She said it was hers by right and that was how it was going to stay. We had a flaming row over it in the end, and that was that."

"I see, sir," said Mole. He waited a moment, then added, "I don't suppose your brother's poor health could have been much of a help to either of them?"

"No, that's true enough," said Tucker. "And it was a great pity. Of course, I tried to help them as much as possible, but mostly they refused any assistance from Blackstock. John had a thing about taking hand-outs, as he called it, especially from us. It was a pig-headed attitude, in my opinion, but that was how he wanted it."

"Tell me, sir, did you agree with your Father's decision?"

The long fingers on Tucker's hands came to a pyramid beneath his chin and he spoke without looking at Mole. "When I first heard of it, I was in Amsterdam on a familiarisation course with one of our Dutch associates, and, yes, I admit I was surprised. My Father had certainly never given any indication of his intentions. But when I returned and heard his explanation of the decision, I thought he was right. In my Father's opinion, I was the one who had the brain to keep Blackstock in business and keep it growing. He believed the place needed vision. John had become no more than a Fen farmer, he said, and Blackstock needed the broader concepts of an international outlook, particularly in view of the country's obvious need to take its place in Europe — the Common Market, Inspector, which my Father foresaw years before it was to become a reality. He was that sort of man." Tucker paused. "Though I'm perhaps the last person who should say it, I am an internationalist when it comes to farming, Inspector. And that's what Blackstock needs." He collapsed the pyramid of fingers to two lightly clenched fists on the desk.

"Well, it certainly seems a busy place, sir," smiled Mole, glancing towards the window and the busy yard beyond. "In spite of not having your brother's land," he added.

"Those fifty acres could be put to excellent bulb growing use," said Tucker sharply. "And that's what they should be doing."

"I'm sure you're right, sir," said Mole, still smiling, then letting his mouth sink into a firmer line. "But to come to the specifics. You say you feel you may be under some suspicion of having murdered Mrs Tucker. I presume this is a feeling based largely on the fact that you had, as you say, a flaming row with her over the future of her farm and because of that I might deduce that you killed her out of spite, or in the hope of being able to more easily get your hands on the land with Mrs Tucker out of the way?" Mole paused. "Have you any idea what will happen to the farm now, sir?"

"None," said Tucker flatly, "except that I suppose it will finish up with one of her brothers who may or may not want it. They're in Canada, you know. But as for your presumptions, Inspector, yes, that's precisely how I feel—and no doubt a few others in Cheal End are thinking along the same lines. Everyone knew of our differences. Not a pleasant situation for me, or my wife."

"I agree, sir, and on the face of it there doesn't look at the moment to be any good reason why you should not have murdered Marcia Tucker—anger and the desire to own something beyond the reach of rational behaviour have been the motives for murder often

34

enough. So let's clear the air. We know that Marcia Tucker was murdered last Friday afternoon between three and five-o'clock. Where were you on that day between those times, sir?"

Here we go again, thought Fisher, as he finished the dregs of the melted ice in his drink, returned the glass to the tray, then flicked to a clean page in his notebook. Any minute now the Inspector will start pacing up and down the room, to a wall and back again, fingering the twists of grey hair in his sideboards, digging his other hand deep into his jacket pocket and nervously turning over some leftover item. Not, Fisher considered, glancing quickly round the room again, that there was much space here for pacing; he'd probably go round in circles instead. It was always the same. Contemplation, Mole called it; impatience was how Fisher described it. And when was Mole going to get himself a new jacket? That brown tweed job he'd worn for the last four years wouldn't raise ten pence at a jumble sale. . . .

As it was, Mole stood perfectly still, his eyes fixed on Tucker's face, his arms folded, his mouth in a still, straight line.

"I was in Moston on that day until five-o'clock," said Tucker, with relief and through a soft smile. "All afternoon, in fact," he added. "I left here at midday."

"Could I have a note of exactly where in Moston you were, sir?" said Fisher in what he thought of as his best courtroom voice.

"Certainly, Sergeant," said Tucker coming to his feet then settling himself on the corner of the desk and swinging his long left leg. "Now let me see . . ." He paused, rubbing his chin and half-closing his eyes in recall. "I had a late breakfast, drove to Moston and reached there about twelve-forty-five, parked the car and did some personal shopping at Hannahs, the bookshop, you know. I had a book on order and wondered if it was in. It wasn't, as a matter of fact. Then

I kept an appointment with my accountant at one-fifteen — Ostridge and Partners, if you want to check. Our business is handled by Samuel Ostridge, whom I met and took to lunch at The George in the High Street. We had roast duckling."

"And then, sir?" said Fisher before Tucker had time to adjust his perch.

"Then, Sergeant, I returned with Mr Ostridge to his office to sign some papers."

"At what time did you leave him?" said Fisher, concentrating on his notes.

"At exactly three-forty-five," said Tucker flatly. "I can be sure of that because Mr Ostridge had another appointment at that time and I kept the client waiting a minute or two, as his receptionist will recall."

"Thank you, sir," said Fisher.

"And from a quarter to four until five?" asked Mole.

"When I left Ostridge's office, I walked through Benn Gate into the Square, noticed the time on the Clock Tower and decided that I had time to browse."

"To browse, sir?" said Fisher, looking up from his notebook.

"Yes, Sergeant, browse. My great interest in life, outside the farm, is books, so I browsed."

"You returned to Hannahs, sir?" said Fisher.

"No, Blockleys, the antiquarian booksellers; and finally I called at Smiths to collect my copy of *Farmer & Stockbreeder*. I left Moston as the Clock Tower struck five."

"And you came straight home, sir?"

"Directly to Blackstock, arriving at shortly after half-past. I had a bath, dressed and took a sherry with my wife before greeting guests for dinner at six-thirty."

"You returned via the Cheal Crossing?" said Mole.

"Yes, Inspector. I always come that way."

"Was there anyone about at that time — anyone you noticed?"

"No, I don't think so . . ." Tucker paused, rubbed his chin again. "No, I'm sure there was no one."

"You travelled by car, of course, sir?" said Fisher.

"Yes, I did. Normally, I take the Jag but on Fridays in Moston it's much easier to park my wife's Mini. I took that. It's out there in the yard." He waved a hand towards the window.

"Well, thank you very much, sir," said Mole, collecting his hat from the desk. "That all seems perfectly satisfactory."

"You mean I'm in the clear?" said Tucker, dropping quickly to his feet and smiling.

"I wouldn't put it quite like that at this point, sir. We shall have to check the details of your movements — pure procedure, you understand — but, yes, I think I can go so far as to say that subject to that check you do not appear to have been in the area at the time Mrs Tucker met her death."

"Well, thank you, Inspector." Tucker let his shoulders relax as he placed his hands on the desk and leaned against it. "I must say that's a relief — although I wish you could communicate your opinions to the rest of Cheal End."

"Can't help there, sir," said Mole. "A bit out of our province."

"Of course," said Tucker. "I didn't expect . . ." He paused, reflected for a moment, then continued, "But tell me, how can you be so sure that I didn't murder Marcia?"

"I can't be sure, sir, but I am quite sure that Mrs Tucker met her murderer at between half-past three and four on that Friday afternoon — and if you were browsing, as you call it, at that time, then I don't see that you have much to worry about."

"I see," said Tucker slowly. "So you think she met someone locally?"

"I didn't say that, sir — but, yes, it seems highly

likely."

"One of those drifters she was always employing."

"Perhaps." Mole paused. "Did she have any gentlemen friends to your knowledge, sir?"

"Gentlemen friends!" mocked Tucker, laughing sardonically. "I'd hardly call any of Marcia's recent friends gentlemen, Inspector. More likely layabouts and hangers-on."

"She had no local acquaintances — of a more intimate nature?" said Mole, disregarding Tucker's sarcasm.

"Not that I knew of, although I didn't keep a close watch on her, you know."

"Quite so, sir."

Tucker turned to the window. "But she had a lousy reputation," he said coldly. "She seemed to go to pieces after my brother's death. Things started to go wrong at the farm — just as I'd warned her they would without help and planning — and she lost heart. Stupid woman! Then she turned to, well, other interests, Inspector." He faced Mole again. "She wasn't quite a whore, but not far short of it. They say she'd sleep with anyone for a week in return for half-a-day's ploughing."

Tucker's mouth screwed to a sneer of distaste. If he could have vomited the words, he would have done so.

"Who are *they*, sir?" asked Mole.

*"Alan! For God's sake!"*

# EIGHT

Neither Mole, Fisher nor Tucker had been aware of the door opening and the slim, slight figure of Helen Tucker entering the room. Mole turned quickly. The voice had been high-pitched, a shrill of anger and disgust; a woman's voice and one belonging to someone of a nervous, even anaemic disposition, thought Mole. Certainly someone who very obviously resented hearing Marcia Tucker referred to as Cheal End's whore. If Mole had expected to see a hand-twisting, face-twiching little hen of a woman, however, ready to peck away at anything that introduced so much as a whiff of circumspect morality into her home, he was mistaken.

Helen Tucker was small, no more than five-feet two or three, with black hair that lay in easy waves to a short, casual style. She was dressed in pale blue slacks and a white nylon blouse through which her tight breasts cast patches of grey shadow. But it was the soft, sensitive features of her face that held the attention. They could never have been composed of simple human flesh and bone, thought Mole; these were the features of a delicately sculptured doll: gentle brown eyes, a small nose whose nostrils seemed to be hidden away, and almost angelic lips. Her skin was tanned to a hint of gold; her whole presence like that of one of the figurines on Tucker's shelves — except that this delight was living and breathing.

"Inspector — my wife, Helen. And this is Sergeant Fisher, Helen." Tucker's introductions were hurried and apologetic as he bustled round the desk, took his wife's elbow and drew her into the room. "I'm sorry, we didn't hear you, Helen." Tucker stared into her face, a gratuitous smile breaking the line of his mouth.

"There was no reason to speak of Marcia like that. No reason at all," Helen Tucker snapped angrily, withdrawing her elbow from her husband's hand and turning to face Mole and Fisher. "It isn't true," she said, a frown appearing beneath a wave of her hair. "It's all horrible, scandalous gossip. No more than you'd expect of some people round here. You're not to believe a word of it, Inspector. You don't, do you?"

"Well . . ." began Mole.

"That poor woman is dead," she went on without hearing Mole, "and what no one seems to realise is that she probably died broken-hearted. She'd lost everything — everything that matters to a woman." She flared defiantly at Mole, at Fisher and then at her husband. "Do any of you understand that?"

Mole looked from Helen Tucker to her husband. He waited a moment, then said: "I don't think anyone is unaware of the hardships Mrs Tucker faced, but that doesn't alter the fact that we are dealing with a murder and one committed in circumstances that do not appear to leave much to the imagination as to what she was doing at Cheal Crossing last Friday afternoon. Regrettably, they appear to be the facts, Mrs Tucker — the sort of facts we cannot walk away from."

"Do you blame her?" asked Helen Tucker bluntly.

"It is not my job either to condone or condemn. I do not sit in judgement on the woman's morals, but I do have the task of probing into them, sifting and sorting them into a picture that begins to make sense and leads to the discovery of her murderer. It may be that in doing so some unsavoury details will emerge. Perhaps I shall discover a lonely woman; perhaps, as you say, a broken-hearted one. Perhaps I shall feel sorry for her, or even come to the conclusion that she brought her death on herself through either her stupidity or over-playing the field. It makes little difference at the moment, Mrs Tucker. She is dead and somewhere there is a murderer going free. I intend to put an end to that freedom at the earliest possible opportunity."

When Mole had finished and a thoughtful silence been drawn across the room — even the noises in the yard had crept away — Helen Tucker bit nervously at her bottom lip and clenched her hands in front of her. The anger in her eyes had subsided and they were softer now, moistened with the glaze of emotion.

40

"I'm sorry, Inspector," she said quietly. "You must forgive me. I'm very upset. This business — it's so awful. I. . ."

"We understand," said her husband, placing an arm across her shoulders. "And I'm sorry too." He turned to Mole. "I should not have spoken as I did. It was ill-considered and cruel."

Mole revolved his hat in his hands, appearing to examine its rim. "More to the point, sir, was it true?"

Alan Tucker remained silent. His arm came away from his wife's shoulder, he sighed and walked to the window, staring into the deep shadows cast by the barns. "God knows," he said at last, shaking his head. "She had everything to live for in a way. There was a lot of future ahead of her. But. . ."

"Yes, it was true!" Helen Tucker's glance darted across her husband's face then settled on Mole. "But not in the way Alan described it."

Mole cleared his throat. "Did you know Mrs Tucker well?"

"Not really — at least, not until after John's death, then we seemed to come closer." She paused. "I suppose it was inevitable. Even so, she was very bitter towards us, particularly Alan and Blackstock, but no doubt Alan's told you of that?"

"Yes," said Mole, "I think I see that side of the picture clearly. What interests me more is the closeness you speak of, Mrs Tucker. How did that come about?"

"After John's death, I naturally felt she needed help — oh, not the sort of help Alan offered, nothing to do with the running of the farm. I thought another woman's closeness might ease the burden — someone to talk to of her feelings, fears and hopes. And at first that worked well enough. We met fairly regularly, mostly at her farm, but sometimes in Moston. She wouldn't have anything to do with Alan, but I never talked farming or land."

"What did you talk of?" asked Mole.

"Mostly it was about John and his illness; sometimes about their hopes; sometimes about the fact that she'd never been able to have children — that had been a terrible blow to them. And sometimes it was about nothing at all — the weather, the home, the shopping, that sort of thing. The fact that we were talking seemed to help, but I never probed."

"Did she ever speak of her — her friends?" asked Mole, noting the flick of Alan Tucker's eyes to him as he hesitated and then abandoned the word gentlemen.

"If by that you mean her lovers!" Helen Tucker began with a snap. "No — no she had few friends," she added more gently. "I know everyone talks of her having been free and easy, but I don't think she was, Inspector. Alright, there may have been a few acquaintances made during her trips to Moston — in fact, I know there were, but don't ask me for names — and yes, I think she may have been close, perhaps very close, to some of them, but Marcia just wasn't the type to put herself on the open market. She was, oh, what shall I say, resilient and contained and a very thoughtful person. I mean, she thought about things and weighed them. She wouldn't have given up completely and, well. . ."

"I see," said Mole, "so as far as you are concerned you do not know of any particular friends of either sex?"

"No, other than the village people, of course, and the casual labour she employed early on."

"Are they known characters?"

"Some of them," said Alan Tucker, moving to his wife's side, "but mostly they're simply drifters. Marcia, unfortunately, could afford only the worst of them — the here today, gone tomorrow types. You never see them again once they've been paid."

Mole nodded. "You were saying, Mrs Tucker, that your closeness to your sister-in-law worked well enough at first. Do I take it that there was a deterioration in your friendship?"

"Yes, there was," she said, walking to the bookcase, her hands fidgeting between themselves. "Oh, it was something and nothing, but well, she seemed after a while to no longer need my company. Understandable enough, I suppose. After all, we only chewed over sorrow when we met, and so I wasn't too worried when I saw less of her. I thought she must be coming out of her darkness and looking for company that didn't know so much about her past, or wasn't so close to her tragedy." She paused. "But if you want my honest opinion, Inspector, I think that was the time she may have been seeing more of whatever friends she had."

"So you saw little of her during the past few months?"

"No more than perhaps once a fortnight, and then only in passing."

"Did you notice any change in her attitude? I mean, was she any less sorrowful, unusually buoyant, or worried?"

Helen Tucker hesitated. She looked down at her hands and pulled them quickly apart.

"I . . ." she began.

There was a tap at the door. "Excuse me," said Tucker, striding to it, opening it and leaning forward to catch the muttered words from beyond. "Of course," he said finally and, turning to Mole, "Look, Inspector, I'm needed in the bulb sheds. Would you mind?"

"Carry on, sir," said Mole. "We're about finished, anyway. And thank you for your co-operation. We'll be in touch."

"Thank you, Inspector," said Tucker. "I'll be back shortly, Helen."

When he had gone, Mole smiled at Helen Tucker. "I'm afraid I'll have to bother you for an account of your movements last Friday afternoon, Mrs Tucker, if it's no trouble."

"Of course," she said, her eyes widening as though

returning from a world of personal thoughts. "I was here — here all day. We had guests to dinner that evening and I was busy preparing for them."

"Thank you," said Mole. "And now I think we'll move on, Sergeant."

"Yes, sir," said Fisher, closing his notebook.

"Again, my thanks, Mrs Tucker."

"Inspector," said Helen Tucker, a chill of urgency in her voice.

"Yes?"

"There is something you should know." She took a step forward. Again her hands writhed between themselves; the moisture in her eyes glistened and her small breasts hardened beneath the white blouse.

Someone has picked up the beautiful figurine, thought Mole, and she does not like it.

"Yes?" he said again.

"Marcia was to have been married."

The words trembled on her unsteady breathing. Then Helen Tucker's eyes closed and she wept in deep, convulsive spasms.

## NINE

"It's odd that, sir," said Sergeant Fisher, taking a swipe at a fly with his notebook and chasing it out of the car's open window. "Very odd." He glared after the fly's flight into the street, slumped back in the seat, then turned the pages of the book until he reached the one he had been reading. "I wonder why Marcia Tucker told her in the first place? And why didn't she say who she was going to marry? That's not like a woman. Doesn't make sense."

Mole sighed. They had left Blackstock and cruised slowly into Cheal End until, reaching the main street, Mole had instructed the driver to pull over to the shadowed side of the road and stop. He had felt in need of "a breather", as he put it; time to collect his thoughts again. He looked round him. It was an ordinary village street, typical of those in the Fenlands, with rows of cottages set flush to the roadside, haphazardly sited bungalows and houses built further back to create a straggle to the line; a general store displaying gaudy discount notices and a selection of vegetables in boxes propped against the frontage; the tin and stainless steel facade of a hardware store, and in the distance, the Five Cats, with its white shuttered windows and scrubbed greystone step at the entrance.

An elderly woman walked towards the car, peering circumspectly at its unfamiliar presence and mysterious occupants; on the other side of the road, a sandy brown labrador lay sprawled in the sun, its flanks heaving, its ears nudging away flies. Behind the car, the church clock struck three. The old woman passed with a last defiant stare, the dog lifted its head as though in recognition of the time, and Sergeant Fisher took another swipe at an intruding fly. Mole sighed again, closed his eyes and wished he were home with a pint pot of beer at his elbow.

"Do you reckon that explains all the clothes she had sir?" said Fisher. "A sort of going away outfit?"

"Could do," grunted Mole, opening his eyes and blinking at the sun's brightness.

Fisher frowned and struggled with his notes. "Who the devil would she have been set to marry? Couldn't have been anyone from here or it'd have been common knowledge. Somebody from Moston, perhaps? But I don't understand why she didn't give his name to Helen Tucker. I mean, you'd think she'd have been only too anxious to talk about him. Never known a woman yet who didn't natter ninety to the dozen about a wedding, especially her own. Course, I suppose it'd have been a quiet affair. Not a church do, you can bet. Registry Office in Moston's my guess. Still, it doesn't explain her silence. But she must have told *somebody*. It's only natural — don't you think so, sir?"

"Hmmm," mused Mole, stretching his legs along the space in the back of the car. "I'm not sure that anything's natural in a case of murder, Sergeant. But I agree, it does seem strange that she didn't make more of it, or at least talk about it. Unless . . ." he paused, his eyes narrowing. "Unless whoever it was she was to marry didn't want it talked about."

"And why would that be, sir?"

"No idea, Sergeant. Just a thought." He stifled a yawn. The day was hot, he was hot, and nothing made sense. "What was it Helen Tucker said?"

Fisher dampened a finger and flicked at his notebook. "Let's see now. She said — ah, yes, here we are — she said: There is something you should know. Marcia was to have been married. Then she broke down. Then you asked her if she could tell you precisely what had been said and when, and she said: It was last Wednesday. We met in Moston, in Blatley's store. We hadn't seen each other for weeks, nearly a month — at least, not to speak to. She was in the store's shoe department. I was looking for a pair of sandals. She saw me, waved and came across. She was smiling and very bouncy, full of herself and chattering on about not being able to make up her mind between blue and grey. And then she put a hand on my arm and said, guess what, I'm getting married. Just like that. I was dumbfounded. I started to say something, then she said she couldn't stop, she'd give me a ring; we'd have a coffee one morning. Then you, sir, asked her if she'd discussed it with her husband. No, she said she hadn't.

46

She thought it would upset him and make him start wondering all over again about what would happen to the farm, and she'd had enough of listening to that. In any case, she knew so little. She wanted to have another word with Marcia before saying anything to anyone." Fisher closed the book. "But she never did, sir — and when she planned to pop over to the farm to see her that week-end, it was too late. Marcia Tucker was dead."

Mole stayed silent, watching the half-asleep dog's ears fending off flies.

"Do you think Helen Tucker believed her, sir? It must have come as a shock."

"She believed her alright. What I want to know is did she have a good idea of who the groom was to be?"

"She said not."

"To us, Sergeant, to us."

"You mean it was someone she knew?"

"Perhaps." Mole stretched, yawned and settled his hat on his head. "It's just after three now, Sergeant. Drop me at Dr Hill's, you have a look round the village, see what local gossip you can pick up, find Charlie Stokes and tell him I want to see him in the morning, then collect me in an hour and we'll drive back to Moston."

"Very good, sir."

"And Sergeant," added Mole, as the car's engine came to life, "find out if there's a local sewing circle, or dressmaking class in the village and if Marcia Tucker ever joined in."

"Yes, sir," sighed Fisher, attacking another fly and sending it buzzing furiously towards the pestered dog.

# TEN

Mole had a passion for impossibly old buildings of gnarled stone, mis-shapen rooms and tipsy roofs that were still lived in. It seemed to him that in making such places work for modern living the owners had to have a sense of history. It was not simply a question of grabbing four walls in both hands, shaking them and hoping that by some lucky twist of design everything would fall into a well-ordered 1970's shape and still remain a glimpse of pure rural charm for which passing motorists would slow down.

You had to touch the place with gentleness, feel its pulse, discover its character; you were blind to its past but your finger-tip appreciation should let you into the tales it had to tell and how it had weathered them. You needed to know every room, every window, door, beam and cranny, stone and nail, as though you were making friends with a wise but weary old man. No need to rush things — let him talk and reminisce. Sooner or later, given understanding for his age and care for his frailty, he would reveal his deepest thoughts of the past and share them with you. Never mind the craggy old face, with its splits and lines and look of another age. It was what went on inside that mattered.

Now take this old man, he thought, as he opened the gate to the Barn and walked slowly up the path to the front door; this old fellow would be two hundred years old if he was a day. Yes, all of that, and he wore his senility like a favourite smoking jacket. The stonework had been cared for, the timbers replaced at the

48

windows, the roof re-slated, but the design of the place had not changed. There had been no architectural indulgence allowed here; the character was untouched and in fine voice. . . .

"Can I help you?"

Mole stopped, turned and peered towards a tangle of shrubs to his left. The voice had no face but seemed close by. He peered harder, raising a hand to his eyes against the strong sunlight.

"If it's a prescription, there's a box at the surgery door. Round the other side."

This time he was able to make out a smudged but smooth skinned face among the deep shadows of the evergreens.

"Doctor Hill?" queried Mole.

"Yes, that's me," said the woman, emerging from the thicket, dusting her hands on the baggy corduroys she wore below a torn man's shirt, and pushing back the brim of a floppy gardening hat.

"Sorry to trouble you, Doctor, I'm Inspector Mole, Moston C.I.D. Could I have a word with you?"

"Oh. Police," she said, coming closer. "I half expected I'd be on your list. It's about Marcia Tucker?"

"Just a routine check. Won't take a minute."

"That's alright, Inspector."

She was about Mole's height and his age, he thought, as she faced him, giving her hands a final rub together, then settling them where her hips pushed the belted trousers into ruckled folds. Mole noticed a fringe of blonde hair beneath the hat, blue eyes, a straight narrow nose, and a cheerful mouth. She was attractive and, he guessed, quite slim beneath the bulge of working clothes. Her gaze was easy and confident, as though waiting with infinite patience to hear of his troubles.

"Shall we go inside? This sun's killing — although I know we shouldn't complain!" She smiled and led the way up the path to the open front door. She slipped off the old shoes, dropped the hat on a table and padded barefoot along the short corridor from the hall that led to a cool, long room hung with pen and ink portraits and furnished with expensive reproduction pieces against a setting of white plastered walls. At the far end of the room, french doors stood open to a small patio beyond which was a lawn and neat flower beds.

"Can I offer you a cup of tea, Inspector?" she said, sinking into an expansive chair and crossing her legs.

"No thank you. I'm in a bit of a hurry as it is."

"Then have a seat."

Mole moved to a chair facing her and sat down. He glanced admiringly around the room.

"You like it?" she asked.

"Very much. I'm a fanatic for old places—have a small cottage of my own at Bird Dyke, nothing quite as grand as this, of course, but I'm always interested to see how other people have adapted a place."

"You didn't say modernise," she smiled.

"No, I don't like that word. It hints of character destruction."

"I agree. You must see the rest of the house."

"I'd very much like to, but at the moment . . ."

She held up a hand. "I can guess—you're in the thick of it! Well, alright, some other time. Now, how can I help?"

Mole sat forward, his elbows resting on his knees, his hat dangling from his hands.

"It's about Marcia Tucker, as you guessed."

"Yes, an incredibly complex affair," she said, lowering her eyes to her folded hands.

Mole was surprised. That was the last reaction he had expected.

"As you say, complex. But I was wondering if, as her doctor. . ."

"How did you know that?" she asked quickly.

"I found this"—he took the prescription from his wallet and handed it to her—"on Mrs Tucker's dressing-table at the farm."

Jeanne Hill read it and handed it back. "She never had it made up," she said, more to herself than to Mole.

"I was hoping you could perhaps tell me why, Doctor?"

She stared steadily at Mole. "Normally, Inspector, I'm against discussing my patients with anyone at any time. And that applies to the dead as well as the living. But in this case, there are certain things which are better said." She unfolded her hands and relaxed them on the chair's arms. "That prescription to begin with—nothing very sinister in that, I can assure you. It's for sleeping-tablets. You will appreciate, that Mrs Tucker had been through a traumatic time with the loss of her husband and was under some considerable strain. She wasn't sleeping at all well when she came to me last April."

"You had treated her husband?"

"No. As you may know, I have not been in Cheal End for very long. By the time I arrived, John Tucker was already under specialist treatment, although I did hear of his case through the hospital in Moston. Mrs Tucker became my patient immediately after her husband's death."

Mole held the prescription lightly in his fingers. "By August, she obviously felt she needed this," he said.

Jeanne Hill was silent, her gaze fixed intently on Mole in a stare of indecision.

Mole waited, then slowly and deliberately replaced the paper in his wallet. "Then something must have happened . . ." he began.

"Something to change her attitude, Inspector? You're right, there was." Again, she paused, this time staring beyond Mole to the wall at his back. Then suddenly, she said, "It's my opinion Inspector, that it

51

was about that time that she met the man she was going to marry."

Mole looked up quickly. "She told you *that?*"

"You already knew?"

"About an hour ago," said Mole through a dryness in his throat.

"I won't ask from whom you heard — I can guess. Helen Tucker?"

"Yes."

"The only other person in Cheal End Marcia seemed to care about — why, I don't understand when you think of the very uncommon ground between them. However. . ."

"When did she tell you of the impending marriage, Doctor?"

"In October."

"Did she say who she was going to marry?" asked Mole anxiously.

"No, that's what bothers me. I asked her point-blank — I was so pleased for her — but all she would say was that for the moment she was keeping it quiet. She didn't want all of Cheal End to have time to chew it over, she said; they'd only make of it what suited them. And in any case, it wasn't any of their business. She was a very determined woman."

Mole slumped back in the chair. "And you wouldn't have any idea who it might have been?"

"None at all — although I doubt if it was anyone in the village. I know most of the people here, Inspector, and frankly I can't think of anyone remotely eligible."

"She never spoke of anyone she was particularly close to?"

"As I say, she seemed to have a relationship with Helen Tucker, and she presumably looked upon me as a friend, which is why she told me about the marriage in the first place, I think. Outside of that, there was no one to my knowledge. But that's not surprising. She was very conscious of her reputation."

Mole replaced the wallet, picked up his hat and turned it in his hands. "Was there any truth in it, do you think?"

"Do you, Inspector?"

"I'm not sure," he sighed. "She must have seemed cast off. She wouldn't sell the farm, but on the other hand she must have known that she couldn't carry it on."

"And between the two, Inspector, was a great loneliness and, I think, a coldness. Let me explain."

She got up and walked towards the french doors. Composed, but with a frown of concentration across her forehead, she said:

"Marcia Tucker was an intelligent and attractive woman. Personally, I'm not at all sure that she should ever have stayed in this area after she left school—she'd probably have done better in a new environment, but that's a personal opinion. She married a farmer and farming became her life, but when the strain and struggle of that ended in the tragic way it did, it's also my opinion that something, call it frustration, even a sense of unidentified freedom, was released. She tried, and tried very hard, to hold on to all that she had spent her life working for, even though she knew it was pointless and beyond her and would never be a success.

"So what happened? When the frustration and feeling for freedom got the upper hand, she broke out in a way totally alien to her nature, her upbringing and, yes, if you like those old-fashioned things called standards. I'm convinced that Marcia had never looked at another man in her life. There had been no need. I think she loved her husband and was devoted to him and the ideal he had, but I also think she felt she owed him something. She could not have children, Inspector, and for her that was, if you like, the final straw. She and John were working for nothing—neither for themselves, nor for a generation to come. Always they were in the vacuum of an empty space — a struggling past, a fight for the present and no horizon to look to. And then John died. . .

"Can you imagine how she must have felt? From having nothing, she passed into having even less, if that's possible. And, yes, that's why she did have a reputation, as they call it — she broke out, Inspector, and for all I know drank and fornicated all over Fenland. But I can assure you that it didn't last. Three months, perhaps four, but not a week longer, I'm positive. Don't ask me how I can be so certain — that's medical training or perhaps just a woman's understanding of another woman. But that phase in her life passed, and she found something new and very tangible to hold on to. She fell in love — at first perhaps regretfully and in a confused way so soon after John's death, then deeply and very passionately; the way, Inspector, that lifts a woman above herself and into another world. For Marcia that was perhaps tenderness, or perhaps security, but above all it was hope. She at last had a future she could see."

She paused and turned back to the open french doors. "You've been asking yourself who that person is who promised so much. I cannot tell you, but what I can tell you is when that new world was to begin."

She turned again to Mole, staring steadily into his eyes.

"Marcia could not have been at Cheal Crossing for the purpose everyone assumes, Inspector. That was to have been her wedding day."

# ELEVEN

There are sausages and sausages but only Evans'
sausages *are sausages*! It was a revelation Inspector Mole
had faced early in life. He loved them, fried, boiled, hot
or cold, on their own or in any combination of
accompanying vegetables. He would, and had, given up
a lot for them; missed an appointment, travelled miles
out of his way in search of them and, he guessed, if the
day of reckoning were to ever come, spent a small
fortune on them. They had satisfied him at the oddest
times of day and night: for breakfast, cold for elevenses,
at lunch, tea, dinner and supper, indoors and outdoors,
alone or in company, not to mention at dawn when,
restless and in deep thought, he had paced the rooms of
his cottage thinking his way through a problem aided
and abetted, he liked to think, by an Evans' sausage.
They were as much a part of his life as his passion for old
houses, tweed jackets, brogue shoes and the scent of
chrysanthemums. But to this day — and he must, he
thought, have been eating them for over forty years — he
still could not define the true "majesty" of their flavour.
Edgar Evans had never revealed the secrets of his recipe.
That, he had always claimed, was something between
him and the gods.

And the gods, thought Mole, clearing the last of his
plate of Evans' sausages and fried tomatoes, had a habit
of keeping an awful lot to themselves. He finished his
mouthful, reached for his pot of draught bitter beer and
settled back in the chair in the private dining room of
the Ship's Side, the only Moston pub able to satisfy his

gastronomic indulgence.

It had been a day of long problems and surprising if incomplete answers, or, as Sergeant Fisher had remarked on their drive back to Moston: "Talk about lifting the muck to discover an orchid . . ." It had been confusing enough to discover that Marcia Tucker had planned to marry — confusing, he reflected, but perhaps not surprising. After all, she had been an attractive woman and there was the farm which might be seen by some as a sizable dowry. Land did fetch a good price . . . Or was he being callous? But then to discover that she was to have been married on the day she was murdered, now that really did, as Fisher had again remarked, "set the cat among the pigeons."

Mole considered himself fortunate to have made contact with Doctor Hill so early in the proceedings and to have heard while it was still so fresh in her memory, Marcia's last known confidence. It was odd, however, that Doctor Hill should have heard of the date on the day that Helen Tucker had been told of the forthcoming marriage, or perhaps it was coincidence. "I was astonished," the Doctor had told him. "Bowled over, in fact. There she stood in my surgery on that Wednesday evening and boldly announced that Friday was to be *the* day. And yet still she wouldn't say who it was — you'll know soon enough, she had laughed, and bounced out of the door as happily as she'd bounced in on some flimsy pretext of having a chill. Why go to all that bother, I asked myself; why not telephone, and why bother to tell me at all if no one was to be invited to the wedding that had an anonymous groom? But there it was, Friday was to be the day. . ."

Then what had happened, pondered Mole, staring into his beer? Between Wednesday night and Friday morning, something or someone of sufficient importance had stopped Marcia Tucker turning up for her own wedding and made her keep an appointment at

Cheal Crossing.

He was at a loss to fathom that one.

But what of the man she was to have married? Who was he, where was he? No one had ever heard of him, much less seen him, and Marcia had never identified him — why? And why had he not come forward? Surely, he wasn't still standing at the Registry Office unaware of what had happened? But for heaven's sake, he frowned, what sort of a man is it who makes an arrangement to marry and then doesn't raise a murmur when his bride is found murdered on their wedding day? Or had the wedding been called off on Wednesday night or Thursday, and if that were the case, again, why? Had that any connection with the appointment Marcia kept at Cheal Crossing? Something had gone very wrong — and it seemed to Mole that it must have occurred during Thursday. "How's that sir?" Fisher had asked. "Clothes, Fisher, clothes. They were still in the wardrobe. Nothing had been packed for the honeymoon. . ."

"Seems to me, sir," Fisher had said when they reached Moston, "that we need to find in double-quick time the man she was going to marry. I reckon he has all the answers — including the reason why he killed her."

Had he, wondered Mole? Was it all that simple — a groom who'd got cold feet and turned in desperation to murder?

He finished his beer, got up and paced quietly round the room.

No, he thought, not even the gods could have dreamed that up. There had to be something else; something or someone somewhere. . . .

His fingers found the thimble in his pocket and he stopped pacing as he examined it for what must have been the twentieth time that day. No good looking there, old son, he murmured to himself. What was it Sergeant Fisher had said: "Yes, sir, there's a sort of sewing bee in the village, run by the Vicar's wife, but not Marcia Tucker's cup of tea. She's never been anywhere near it. . ."

He replaced the thimble and returned to his pacing. Then what about Charlie Stokes? "Not much there, by the sound of it. He's a nice enough bloke," Fisher had reported, "a bit dim witted and half scared out of his life. Says he'd never seen anyone — let alone Mrs Tucker — at the Crossing. It was his hideaway. Anyway, I've fixed for you to have a word with him in the morning."

Mole sighed, turned and paced back along the room. He doubted if Alan Tucker had much more to tell him, and his account of his afternoon in Moston on Friday had seemed satisfactory, but perhaps Helen Tucker might be persuaded to talk more about her relationship with Marcia, as might Doctor Hill. He liked her, he smiled to himself. Yes, she was his sort of woman. . . .

There was a knock at the dining-room door and Mrs Littledyke, the landlord's wife, bustled in, rubbing her hands in the folds of the neat gingham apron at her homely waist.

"Sorry to bother you, Inspector — oh, but you've finished. Then that's alright, 'cus Sergeant Fisher's here and wants a word with you. I'll send him through."

"Thank you, May," said Mole. He had known her long enough and relished sufficient of her cooking of Evans' sausages to be on first name terms. "That was excellent."

"Good, good." She bustled out of the room calling to Sergeant Fisher as she went. "Alright, Sergeant, he's finished."

"You eaten, Fisher?" said Mole when Fisher had closed the door behind him.

"Not yet, sir. Wanted to catch you first, then I'm going for a pie and a pint."

"And some sleep?"

"Maybe," said Fisher, easing himself into a chair and stretching out his legs. "Don't mind admitting I could do with some. Anyway, sir"—he sat up straight again—"three things. First, the Super called . . ."

"Oh, no!" sighed Mole. "Not that!"

"Afraid so, sir," said Fisher, stifling a grin. "Superintendent Hayes 'phoned and said to tell you. . ."

"That he and the Chief Constable would appreciate a chat with me up at The House . . ." mocked Mole.

"Precisely, sir."

"When?"

"Before nine, if possible. It's just after eight now, sir."

"Alright, Sergeant. And?"

"Well, sir, I thought you'd be interested to hear what young Baxter's come up with. I've had him on checking round Moston all day on the reputation Mrs Tucker had here. He's come up with some very useful items."

"I'm listening," said Mole, turning from Fisher and pacing to the end of the room.

"Seems she was a bit of a live wire round the pubs a few months ago—The Swan, The Black Bull, The Red Lion, they all had her at one time or another. Usually with a crowd of fellows."

"Sleeping around?"

"No one can say for sure, sir, but they'd none of them be surprised if she was. Wasn't too choosey about the company she kept—all sorts, drifters, drop-outs, drunks, young and old, it didn't seem to matter. Then it all stopped."

"Stopped?" Mole turned and stood still.

"Yes, sir. Suddenly, no one saw her—and haven't since. One night she was all swinging, the next— nothing. She might have disappeared off the face of the earth."

Mole frowned. "Well?"

"Well, sir, Baxter used his nut for once and decided

to widen his field. He made inquiries at The George and The Royal and found that she'd moved up from the public bars to the cocktail lounges, and the drifters and drop-outs had been replaced by gentlemen known to both of us. Mark Gerson, the jeweller, and Steven Robins, the solicitor. Neither of them married, as you know."

"Interesting," said Mole, returning to his pacing. "I want to see both of them in the morning."

"Yes, sir. Baxter established that she was seeing Gerson at The George and Robins at The Royal, twice a week for the pair of them, usually in the evenings for dinner. And no expense spared."

"Good for Baxter," said Mole.

"I'll let him know, sir," said Fisher flatly. "We'll make something of him yet."

Mole smiled to himself before turning back to Fisher. "And thirdly?"

"Ah yes, sir," said Fisher, brightening. He came to his feet. "I've checked with the Moston Registry Office and there were no weddings at all last Friday, and no cancellations. Of course, Mrs Tucker may have been getting married somewhere else. We're working on that now."

"Good."

"And it so happens," Fisher continued, "that I know the manager at Hannahs bookshop, so I rang him at home to check Alan Tucker's story that he called there last Friday. I thought it'd save a bit of time. We'll have to check the details of his other movements tomorrow."

"And?"

"Well, sir, it's as he said. He did have a book on order at the shop and he did call there on Friday at about the time he mentioned to ask if it was in — but that's what confuses Mr Hannah. You see, sir, Tucker didn't place the order for the book until the previous Monday, and he knows as well as Mr Hannah that it takes all of a fortnight for an ordered book to be delivered. So Hannah was a bit surprised when he called on Friday. He must have known it wouldn't be there, and what bothers Hannah is that Tucker was a bit ratty about it."

"Ratty?"

"Yes, sir, you know — making a scene, taking a swipe at the delay, that sort of thing."

"Drawing attention to himself?"

"Exactly, sir." Fisher drew a long breath. "Creating an alibi, if you ask me."

Mole frowned again.

"I mean," Fisher went on, "it's as if he knew we'd be checking his movements at some time. Don't you think so, sir?"

Mole was silent. He slid his hands deep into his trousers pockets and stared up at the beamed ceiling. What now, gods, he whispered to himself.


## TWELVE

Lieutenant-Colonel F. J. ("Freddy") Bartram, D.S.O., in no way fulfilled the popular image of the professional military man. To begin with, Mole had always thought of him as being too small (five-feet five) to carry the weight of authority, and his twig-like leanness did nothing to give him an air of presence. He could so easily be overlooked, in much the same way that an empty fireplace would pass unnoticed in a room in mid-Summer. Nor did he have any distinguishing features: an almost bald head, peanut eyes, pecky nose, and thin lips — all the ingredients, some had remarked, of a once snappy ferret bristling old fur at the future.

True, he was still very active in retirement and had a habit of darting about as though caught in some skirmish in the steaming foothills of the Punjab. But if Freddy Bartram lacked physical power and attraction, his voice more than compensated for these failings. It was not harsh or booming; neither too fast nor too slow, but as cutting as a laser beam and just about as deadly. A voice that could be comforting, even condescending, were it not for the electric shock that lurked behind every word; a voice that immediately set him apart from other men and stamped him as a leader.

You did not hear his voice, you listened to whatever it was saying and paid attention. Mole had quickly learned the lesson in the eight years or so he had been officially associated with Bartram. Now he thought he knew him, even to the point of predicting his opening remarks whenever they met. "Ah, Mole!" Bartram would say. "Still digging!" And he would laugh and Mole would laugh, and Mole would wish for the thousandth time that Freddy Bartram were not the Chief Constable and could be told that this particular exploitation of his name was a part of history. As it was, he would swallow hard on the sherry that was always offered and stand perfectly still while Bartram darted about, breaking down Mole's latest case into what he termed the "pieces of its strategy."

Nevertheless, thought Mole as he turned the Hillman into the drive to The House and noted that it was two minutes to nine, it was some compensation to have a Chief Constable who cared enough to get involved, albeit that it was only on occasions of major crime that they ever met. He shuddered at the prospect of a crime wave ever hitting the Moston area. Imagine what that would do for the voice!

"Good of you to make it at short notice, Arthur," smiled Superintendent Hayes pleasantly as he led Mole down the hall to the familiar double doors of the dining-room. "How's it going?"

"Grim," said Mole, attempting to straighten his crumpled jacket and shifting it across his shoulders.

Hayes stopped at the doors. "Freddy's really got the bit between his teeth with this one." He raised his eyes in descriptive despair. "There'll be no holding him till you've made an arrest. Any prospects?"

"None," said Mole flatly but truthfully.

"Keep at it," said Hayes, putting his hands to the door handles. "It's early days yet. Come on. I'll try to keep this brief."

"I'd appreciate that, sir," sighed Mole, and followed him into the room.

"Ah, Mole!" Bartram shot out of his chair like a sudden salvo and sped in Mole's direction, hands held forward as though shaping himself into a projectile. "Still digging!" He laughed, Mole laughed, Hayes laughed—and in the few seconds of silence that followed, the echo of the joke was as weak as the struggling smiles on their faces.

"This one smells," said Bartram, moving to a small table on which sherry glasses and a decanter had been placed. "I'd say it's the nastiest case of murder we've had, wouldn't you, Mole?"

"I can't recall one much. . ."

"Nasty!" snapped Bartram, handing round the drinks. "Sex at the bottom of it, I suppose?"

"Hard to say, sir," Mole began.

"Not for me, Mole. Not for me." He sampled his drink. "Put me in the picture."

Bartram darted to the fireplace and stood with his back to it. His small, pin-sharp eyes stared into Mole's without appearing to blink. He waited, poised like an impatient warrior, for a briefing from the war-torn front. . .

Mole was glad of the chance to talk. Whatever he had to say would, he knew, be listened to; every word analysed, scrutinised and shaken out for specks of incriminating dust. But if he kept it going long enough and at his pace, the chances were that the Superintendent might bail him out on the pretext of some urgent enquiry.

"So there we are, sir" he said twenty minutes later, having gone slowly and methodically through the day's events and movements. "There's no doubt about it being a case of carefully planned murder. Who Marcia Tucker was to have married, we have not yet been able to ascertain, but I think we're close."

Mole sipped at his drink, his eyes fixed on Bartram's face, his ears primed for the flak of comment that was sure to come. But surprisingly, Bartram did not counter with his usual flurry of questions and comment. He remained silent and perfectly still by the fireplace, his sherry hardly touched.

"Not quite," he said at last, placing his glass on the mantleshelf. He turned back to Mole and Hayes, a paleness spreading across his face. Then he sank into his chair. "Not quite. You see, for once I think I can add some useful evidence."

Mole frowned. Hayes opened his mouth to speak, but thought better of it. Bartram looked at them, from one to the other, a nerve in his left cheek kicking behind the flesh.

"This isn't easy for me," he began, staring into the fireplace. "But I've waited until I had you here together before saying anything." He paused, seeking inspiration in the charred, empty hearth, then went on, "As you know, I am a member of various clubs and organisations in Moston, a role I do not play too well these days — age creeps inevitably on, gentlemen — but I do keep up some of the more important associations, partly out of regard for my position and partly out of personal interests and, of course, the chance of meeting people. I have many friends, some of them of many

64

years standing, others quite new. But one of the longest friendships I have enjoyed is that of Henry Layton." He looked to Hayes and Mole for recognition of the name. "You know of him well enough, I'm sure. One of the biggest landowners in the county. Well, Henry and I have been good friends ever since I came to Moston. He's a deal younger than me, but that's never been any bar to our sharing common interests and opinions, so much so that over the years we've spent many hours in each other's company. Of late, however, Henry has not been the happiest of men. About eighteen months ago, his wife — a charming woman, I've always thought — had a reckless affair with some upstart of a young business fellow in London. Oh, nothing to threaten the marriage, you'll understand, more of a heatwave in middle-age, you might say — freakish, a bit like this weather. Margaret — Henry's wife — was flattered and swept off her feet somewhat, but it all ended after a few months and everything returned to normal. At least, I thought so, and so did a lot of others — it was common enough talk at the time. But Henry, it seems, had taken the affair closer to heart than anyone imagined. And in some idiotic moment of what I can only assume to be an overdose of self-pity, he took up with a woman here in Moston . . ."

Mole's eyes had never left Bartram's face, but now they wandered thoughtfully to the dark windows at his back. He knew what was coming. . . .

"Marcia Tucker," snapped Bartram, half in anger, half in the pity of childlike self-consciousness. "Apparently they met at an hotel in the town one evening, three or four months ago, I believe. And, well, not to put too fine a point on it, gentlemen, began an affair. Henry would pick her up in Moston and they'd drive, heaven knows where and . . ."

"He's told you all this, sir?" asked Mole.

"Oh, yes, made no bones about it. He came to see me

this morning—shaking all over, looking like death, half demented with the thought that sooner or later you, Mole, would trace some of Mrs Tucker's movements to him."

"Inevitably, sir," said Hayes conclusively.

"Quite so, Superintendent. But there's worse. It's not just simply a matter of their association—that's bad enough, but may or may not be significant. What's more important is the blackmail letter he received last Tuesday."

Hayes looked to Mole, met his eyes and in a quick narrowing of his own made a silent wince. Mole remained silent.

"It's the sort of thing you chaps have seen many times before—a quick paste and scissors job of words from a newspaper, posted in the town on Monday."

"What were the demands, sir?" said Mole.

"Much as you'd expect. Five thousand pounds or Layton's wife would hear of what had been going on. I forget the exact wording, but I've got the letter here."

"He made no attempt to pay?" asked Mole.

"Oh, yes, he was quite prepared to pay up, so he says. Five thousand pounds to Henry Layton would hardly put him on the breadline. He assumed that the letter had come from Marcia Tucker, so drove over to the farm that same evening and confronted her with it."

"She admitted sending it?"

"No she damned well didn't, Mole! She said she hadn't sent the letter and thought the whole thing was a malicious attempt to ruin not only him, but her. She told Layton the best thing he could do was burn the letter and forget all about it."

"Did he believe her?"

"At first, no. He thought it was all part of some ritual she was playing out, making him squirm on the hook. But then she told him of the wedding—and that, of course, convinced him that she hadn't sent the letter.

No question."

"She didn't mention . . ." began Mole.

"A name, Inspector? No, at least, not in full. But what she did say will more than interest you in view of what you've been telling me tonight. Layton was quite clear — she kept repeating that Steve mustn't get to hear of the letter or it'd ruin everything."

"Steve . . ." muttered Hayes. "Steve who?"

Mole continued to stare into the blackened window at Bartram's back. "At a guess," he said slowly, "Steven Robins, her solicitor."

"And I think," said Bartram, easing himself from his chair and bringing the decanter to their glasses, "that you'd be absolutely right, Mole."


# THIRTEEN

Mole slept fitfully, tossing beneath the single sheet until he somehow contrived to wind it round his legs and body and mummify himself. The heat of the night was almost as bad as that of the day, except that the darkness turned it to a glue of thick air through which his every movement wallowed in a slow, sticky motion. He would drift into a troubled sleep of flickering images of dykes, fields, farms and faceless men at church doors, then wake with a sudden jump, perspiration trickling down his neck and across his shoulders. At five, he gave up the struggle, dressed and shaved, made a pot of tea, and rang the Duty Sergeant at Moston.

"Tell Fisher I'll pick him up at the Post Office on the Grimswold Road at eight sharp. We'll be heading for Cromford, Henry Layton's farm. I want to know exactly where I can contact Steven Robins, the solicitor, at about eleven, so have someone keep an eye on him."

At six-thirty, Mole walked into his greenhouse where the temperature was already climbing into the seventies at the start of another scorching day. He pottered absent-mindedly, his mind wandering through the meeting with Bartram and the questions he wanted to ask both Layton and Robins when he got to them. At seven-fifteen, he collected his jacket and hat, brought the Hillman from the shade of the garage and drove out of Bird Dyke in the direction of Grimswold, thankful to have only the mundane emptiness of the open road on which to concentrate. . .

"That's a shaker sir," said Fisher, adjusting the sun shield above his head and watching the grey ribbon of bone dry road swing to the left. "If Marcia Tucker didn't send the letter to Henry Layton, then who did?" He looked quickly across at the silent, frowning Inspector. "Must've been the murderer, or is it a case of a blackmailer who tried it on only to find that someone had beaten him to it? The mind boggles!" He blinked at a sudden sun-spot ahead. "And what about Robins? If he's the missing groom, then what the hell's his game? Makes you wonder, sir, if we shouldn't be heading in the other direction and bringing him in."

Mole concentrated on overtaking a heavily laden lorry, then eased back in his seat. "The fact that Robins hasn't come forward suggests two things, Fisher. One, he isn't the man Marcia Tucker was planning to marry; two, he is the missing groom and is hoping no one will find out."

"In which case, sir, if it's number two, he must be our man."

"Why?" asked Mole.

"Well, sir, if he was going to marry Mrs Tucker and then for some reason changed his mind, whatever that something was didn't go down well with the bride-to-be.

And, hey presto, the ultimate: eliminate bride-to-be and the change of mind is no problem."

"And what do you think could have changed his mind?"

"Heaven knows, sir. Who's to say? Something he found out about her; something he suddenly realised he couldn't live with — there's no telling. Many's the man who's found himself wed only to wish he were dead! It's true, sir. I mean, you take these two: him a solicitor, and her — well, I don't know what you'd call Mrs Tucker, but at best she did have a reputation and she had lived it up and she did own a farm on its last legs. And put all that together, sir, and I reckon you have a problem, the sort of problem Steven Robins may not have wanted as a dowry."

"Surely he'd have had time to find out about these things."

"Not necessarily so, sir," said Fisher philosophically, spreading his legs forward. "First flush of passion and all that. You don't always see what's in front of you." Fisher leaned forward, his eyes half closed. "You see what you want to see, and that's a fact, moreso when it comes to a woman. Turn here, sir."

Mole changed gear and swung sharp left into a narrow lane.

"Straight on now, sir, for about a mile. Grimswold's on the right."

"Alright," said Mole, "then supposing he is our man and did murder Marcia Tucker. What about the blackmail letter?"

"Coincidence, sir," said Fisher, "pure chance. Like I said, someone saw the opportunity of a quick quid or two, but too late."

"Layton's not dead. He could still be blackmailed."

"True enough, sir, but it's my experience that your blackmailer needs a situation. With Mrs Tucker out of the way, who's to say that Henry Layton did or did not have an affair with her? No, sir, whoever it was tried the blackmail angle missed the bus, so to speak."

"And Mark Gerson?"

"Oh, the jewellery chap. No problem there. Just one of the crowd, I reckon."

Mole was silent for a moment. "So it's your deduction, Sergeant, that Steven Robins murdered Marcia Tucker because of a change of mind about marrying her?"

"In a nutshell, sir — yes. It makes sense."

"Which leaves us with the man we're about to meet — Henry Layton."

"Ah, no, sir, not Mr Layton. Not the type. No, sir, he'd have bought his way out of any trouble, you can be sure of that."

"Alright, then, your theory still doesn't explain Alan Tucker's odd behaviour at the bookshop."

"Nor does it, sir. But I think we'll find an explanation for that without too much trouble."

"But surely Robins must have realised that we'd discover his wedding plans sooner or later?"

"Ah, but as you yourself have said on many occasions, sir, these murderers are clever folk. Robins doesn't need to do or say anything at the moment, does he? I mean, we're not asking, are we, sir? And we're driving in the opposite direction to see a man who was *nearly* blackmailed. He hasn't much to worry about, has he, sir?" Fisher relaxed in his seat, a soft and somewhat lofty smile barely discernible on his face.

Mole grated the gears as he steered the Hillman through the village High Street.

"Now where?" he snapped, as they came to a junction.

"Straight on, sir," said Fisher, the smile breaking silently.

# FOURTEEN

Cromford wore its century of life as a country residence with all the geniality of a gentle duke. It stood in the flat landscape like a handsome sculpture in rich brown stone, its windows facing East, its roof tiled in blue slate, its large and ornate entrance at the end of the driveway offering a beckoning welcome to the visitor. Neat, well tended gardens fronted the house, a paddock ran alongside its Southern wing, and trees—oak, beech, pine and sycamore—surrounded it in what, at first glance, appeared to be an outer building of sheltering sentinels. It was the trees as much as anything in the otherwise bare landscape that set Cromford apart as a Fenland home.

Here, thought Mole as he parked the Hillman in the shade by the paddock, is an oasis. He stood gazing along the house frontage, taking in the detail, admiring the care with which the place had been preserved, when, from the corner of his eye, he noticed a figure approaching. There was no mistaking the Harris tweed jacket, riding boots and jodphurs, checked cap and cream silk scarf at the neck. This was the area's wealthiest landowner—Henry Layton.

"Good morning, sir," smiled Mole.

"Mornin'," said Layton, striding out to join them.

"I'm Inspector Mole and this is Sergeant Fisher. I believe you were expecting us?"

"Yes—yes, of course."

He came to within a few feet of Mole and Fisher and stopped, tapping a riding crop rhythmically at his side and staring intently into their faces.

Somewhere in his early sixties and as well preserved as his house, thought Mole, as he scanned the round face with its generous nose, deep set eyes and abrupt chin. Normally, this face would have been jovial, even carefree, with a twinkle of laughter deepening the creases around the eyes and mouth. But now it was set, grim with worry and a tiredness that came of sleepless nights.

"Bartram send you?"

"Yes, sir," said Mole. "He put me in the picture last night and suggested it might be useful if we met."

"Quite so." Layton quickened the tapping. "You know the story?"

"Most of it, sir. There's just one or two points I'd like to discuss."

"Shall we go indoors, or would a stroll round the paddock suit you?"

"Out here's fine, sir. The shade is very pleasant."

"Then we'll walk along the line of the trees."

They had walked in silence for almost a minute before Mole spoke.

"You met Marcia Tucker earlier this year, sir?"

"Yes. I was feeling a bit low at the time for reasons Bartram has no doubt explained to you. Oh, it was . . . well, a damned stupid thing to do, I realise that now. But there we are, it happened. I felt sorry for her. She was such an attractive young woman — far too young to have suffered so much."

"What sort of a relationship developed between you?"

Layton's deep set eyes narrowed until they were no more than black slits. "If you mean . . ."

"I don't mean anything, sir," said Mole. "I am simply asking what it was that held you together."

Layton's face relaxed. "You're quite right to ask, of course. You have to know that if anything else is to make sense. Well . . ." He tapped the crop at his side, then held it tightly in both hands. "At first I thought it was going to be no more than a purely physical relationship, and to be perfectly frank, Inspector, I pursued it along those lines. I needed that sort of closeness at that time, and I thought Marcia did too. But it didn't work out like that at all. To put it bluntly, the physical side of things never amounted to anything more than a kiss and a cuddle. And I'd better be honest — I did try for more, but she said it would spoil everything."

"Did you know of her reputation, sir?" asked Mole.

"Not at first. That was something I learned of later. But it neither surprised nor bothered me, and when I mentioned it to Marcia, she just laughed."

"When did you last meet her?"

"That was on September 15th. The next time I saw her I confronted her with the blackmail letter and accused her of having sent it."

Layton walked towards the paddock fence, then turned to face Mole and Fisher.

"You had no doubt in your mind that she had sent it?" said Mole.

"That was my immediate reaction," said Layton, leaning back on the fence. "I thought perhaps she'd fallen on hard times or something and was using me as a way of raising money, although I was shocked to think that this might be the case. It wasn't her style somehow, and I thought we'd meant more to each other as friends than for blackmail to be the outcome."

"So you decided to face her, sir?"

"Immediately. I went to the farm that evening, found her there and showed her the letter. Before she could say anything, I told her I'd pay — in fact, I'd double what she was asking if she needed money that badly."

"And?"

"She flared up like something on fire! She was absolutely furious — said how could I ever believe that she'd stoop to such a thing, even think of it, and that she

73

didn't need money, mine or anyone else's. Then she seemed to calm down and said she could guess what was happening. Someone was trying to ruin her forthcoming marriage. I was bowled over at that news! It was the first I'd heard of it. But she wouldn't say any more, except that if Steve found out everything would be over. Then she told me to burn the letter."

"Did she have any idea who might have sent it?"

"She said she had, but she could take care of it. But she mentioned no names."

"Then you left her?"

"No, we had a cup of coffee and I apologised for thinking she had sent the letter. I urged her to forget the whole thing and tried to bring the conversation round to her wedding. But she was not interested in telling me more. She said I would hear all about it soon enough. Then I wished her well and hoped that we might meet again soon."

Layton paused, frowned deeply, and looked away from Mole towards the house. "Now, of course, I'm convinced that she did make an approach to the blackmailer and . . . well, met her death as a result of it."

"Hmmm," murmured Mole. He gazed round him, letting his thoughts move through the shadows towards the bright, burned open stretch of the paddock. "And you've no idea who might have sent the letter, sir?"

"I've thought a lot about that, Inspector, and quite honestly I have absolutely no idea. Obviously, it must have been someone who had either seen me with Marcia or at least knew of our relationship. But to my knowledge, no one was aware of our meetings. I certainly never told anyone!"

"Did Mrs Tucker ever mention anyone to you—not an enemy necessarily, a friend perhaps?"

"I know she was friendly with the local doctor, and I think that from time to time she saw her brother-in-law's wife. She had little time for Alan Tucker, as you probably know."

They turned and began to walk back towards the house.

"She had never mentioned Steve until that night?" said Mole.

"Never."

"Other men?"

"None."

"Tell me, sir, did Mrs Tucker ever discuss the farm with you — what she planned to do with it?"

"Only once. It was just before we stopped seeing each other. She said she knew she'd have to sell sooner or later, but she was determined Alan Tucker wouldn't get his hands on it. I disagreed with her on that and pointed out that if the price was right, it mattered little to her who farmed it in the future. But at that time she had no plans to sell. In some strange way, she seemed to be convinced that something would turn up. And I suppose something did."

"In what way, sir?"

"Well, I can only assume that whoever she was going to marry would either want to farm the land or at least have a say in its sale."

"Yes, sir, you're probably right. Well, thank you very much for your help, it's been most useful. Let me know immediately if you receive any further letters, although frankly, I doubt it. All I need to know now, sir, is where you were last Friday afternoon."

"Then I'm a suspect?" said Layton.

"Almost everyone associated with Mrs Tucker is under scrutiny at the moment, sir."

"Yes, of course. Well, Inspector, I was here at Cromford all that day. I think my wife and staff will confirm that."

"You did not leave the premises at all, sir?"

"No. We were supposed to be meeting a buyer for

some of our horses that afternoon, but at about four-o'clock he telephoned to say he couldn't keep the appointment."

"Thank you, sir," said Mole. "One last point, does your wife know of your association with Mrs Tucker—and about the letter?"

They had reached the car and Layton stood staring beyond Mole, an expression of drained relief softening his face. He looked physically and mentally exhausted.

"Yes, she does," he said slowly. "After seeing Bartram yesterday, I decided to tell her the full story." He paused, turned to Mole and smiled softly. "I'm a fortunate man, Inspector. Margaret understands and . . . well, we shall be fine now."

"Good," said Mole, almost as thankful as Layton that the outcome should be so gentle. "I'm sure you're right,"

"Excuse me, sir," Fisher interrupted, "but I think someone is trying to catch our attention."

Mole peered into the bright sunlight towards the entrance to the house where the dark silhouette of a figure waved anxiously at them.

"It's Slingsby, my manager," said Layton.

"Telephone for Inspector Mole!" the man shouted.

"You can take it in my study, Inspector," said Layton, leading Mole and Fisher along the drive to the house.

"Well, thank you again, sir," said Mole as he closed the study door and joined Henry Layton and Sergeant Fisher in the hall. "We'll be on our way now. One or two urgent matters to attend to in Moston. I'll be in touch should there be any developments. Thank you."

Mole dug a prompting index finger into Fisher's back and flicked his eyes towards the door.

"Yes, thank you, sir," said Fisher. "A lovely place you have here . . ."

"Thank you, Inspector, Sergeant," began Layton as

Mole and Fisher ran down the few steps to the drive and headed for the Hillman.

"Trouble, sir?" said Fisher, slamming the door.

Mole brought the car to life, thrust it into gear and was already at the end of the drive and looking anxiously for a clear turning to the right before Fisher could manage another word.

"What's up, then?"

"That was Baxter from Moston," said Mole flatly. "They've just found Charlie Stokes' body in the dyke at the Cheal Crossing."

"Murdered?"

"Stabbed!" snapped Mole.

Seconds later the Hillman was no more than a black speeding dot in a whirl of grey dust.

## FIFTEEN

Charlie Stokes died, as he would have wished, with his boots on. .

Bert Deakin had what he considered a comfortable job for his age and talents; nothing spectacular, but useful work and well enough paid to keep a roof over his head, a meal under his belt and the promise of a pint at the end of the day. After all, it wasn't everyone who would take kindly to "dyking and ditching", as he called it, or to be more exact, working as one of the team of Council labourers who kept the dykes and roadsides of Fenland in a clean and tidy order. Bert liked the work, and after nearly twenty years had succeeded in adjusting the job to his needs and satisfaction. "I works where I wants, when I wants, and th' Council knows it gets a good job done." And it was true. Bert Deakin came and went and did his job along the highways and byways around Cheal End, Fosbrick and Cheal Gate according to the standards he had set. If he saw a dyke in need of attention while on his way to another job one day, he would attend to it the next. If someone mentioned over a pint at the Five Cats that a roadside was in need of trimming, Bert would see to it — just as he had promised he would tidy up the dyke at the Cheal Crossing.

Not that it was overgrown, but the drought, the traffic, the comings and goings of police cars and ambulances, had combined to scatter the dried earth over the tarmac and give it what Alf Sloan, landlord of the Five Cats, had described as an untidy look. And if there was one thing Bert Deakin could not abide, it was untidiness.

He had been at work with a large broom, sweeping away the dirt in pothering clouds of dust, for nearly an hour when, about thirty yards from the Bridge, he had stopped to mop his brow and light a pipe. As the dust clouds settled and Bert concentrated on the flickering match flame over his pipe, he spotted what at first glance appeared to be a man's battered cap lying in the growth about half-way down the dyke. He had waited until the pipe bowl glowed, then, with his instinctive feeling for tidiness, had slithered into the dyke cursing quietly to himself at the wastefulness of the world.

But long before Bert reached the cap, he could see that it had a head in it. The face was white, the eyes staring, the mouth contorted into a twisted grimace. Blood had congealed on one side of the neck into a gluttonous mound that spread like an arm of lava into the dried grass.

"It's bloody Charlie!" was all Bert had gasped.

"After ten and before midnight is my guess," said Archie Tombes to Mole as they watched the body being lifted from the dyke to the waiting ambulance. "And I don't think he was killed here," he continued in that same clinical tone of indifference he used whenever he had to leave his beloved Pathology Department in Moston to examine a dead body.

He rolled down his shirt sleeves and buttoned the cuffs. "Looks to me as if he was dumped here — perhaps from a car or van. You can see the scuff marks from his boots. There." He pointed to two lines of scraped earth.

"Similar weapon?" asked Mole.

"Same one as that used on the Tucker woman, I shouldn't wonder. A repeat performance — quick stab in the neck. You're probably looking for the same killer."

Mole sighed and pushed his hat to the back of his head.

"He must have got in the way," said Tombes. "Might have done more than just discover the Tucker body — might have seen the killer at work." He smiled. "Still, that's your problem, Arthur. I'll let you have a full report by this afternoon."

"Thanks," said Mole and turned his gaze back to the spot where Charlie had been dumped. He eased himself down the dyke side and parted the growth around where the body had lain. He had no idea what he was looking for; it was a forlorn hope that there might be something, anything, that hinted at who had killed Charlie.

Fisher joined him. "What's the next move, sir?" he asked quietly.

Mole did not look up as he scrummaged through the parched grass and earth. There was nothing — nothing save dust and dried blood and hot earth and the feel and smell of death. He took his handkerchief from his pocket and mopped fitfully at his brow. "The next move?" he croaked. "Well now, let's see shall we, Sergeant — let's just bloody well see!"

Mole scrambled back to the road, hot, irritated and

frustrated. He should have known, had at least some inclination that Charlie Stokes had either seen or heard something in the past which had fixed the possible killer of Marcia Tucker in his mind. Why hadn't he thought of and sensed the possibility? It was the heat, it was dulling his senses. His lips came together in a tight line.

"I want that solicitor fellow, Steven Robins," he said to Fisher, turning his stare deep into the Sergeant's sweating face. "I want him within the hour—in Moston, in my office!"

"Yes, sir. I'll get on with it right now!"

"And I want this village sealed up, Sergeant! I want it as tight as a drum! I want to know who goes in, who comes out, where they come from, where they're going to. When Cheal End turns on a tap, I want to know!" He watched the rivulets of sweat on Fisher's face trickle into his thick neck. "Do your best, Sergeant," he added, a hint of a smile round his eyes.

"Yes, sir," said Fisher. "Leave it to me. What about you?"

"I'm going into the village."

"I'll get the car up, sir."

"No, I'll walk, Sergeant. I need to walk—even in this heat. Take the Hillman, then pick me up in half an hour or so. Oh, by the way, where did Charlie Stokes live?"

"In one of the Stone Cottages, sir. Number five, you can't miss it. Opposite the pub."

"Did he live alone?"

"No, sir, with his parents. They're a pretty aged pair."

"Right. Get to it, Sergeant!"

Fisher waited until the Inspector was out of ear-shot before turning to the group of Constables gathered round the three cars at his back. "Alright!" he bellowed. "Let's break up the party and look lively! You there, Simmons . . ."

Mole walked at an even, contemplative pace for nearly ten minutes, crossed the bridge at the Crossing and was on the outskirts of Cheal End before his irritation subsided and he felt able to think clearly.

He passed the silent Tucker farm, the driveway to the bustle of Blackstock, and walked deeper into the village. His frown had mellowed, but his eyes were still fierce.

The Stone Cottages were aptly named, for that is what they were: dull, yellow cottages packed into a single block of eight facing the Five Cats. They were small, tight, darkened boxes from which their windows stared tiredly onto the brightness of the day. Each had a small front door opening directly onto the road; each a four-paned window to the right of the door, and above that a similar window that looked out from a bedroom. They were old and in need of repair, their paintwork peeling and strafed by the Fenland winds, their doorsteps sunken and chipped from the passage of generations of families. They were a reminder of an age that had passed and yet testimony, if such were needed, to the certainty of the future.

Number five was no different from its neighbours, except that here the curtains were drawn. Mole knocked quietly at the door and listened keenly for sounds of life behind it.

When the door was opened it revealed the lined, unshaven face of an old man dressed in baggy brown trousers, collarless crumpled shirt, fat-stained waistcoat and battered check slippers. His long fingers curled fearfully round the door's edge as he peered through the narrow gap at Mole.

"Mr Stokes?" said Mole gently.

The man simply nodded.

"Inspector Mole, Moston CID. Could I see you for a moment?"

The man stepped back and Mole moved into the dim

and cluttered parlour.

A large table covered with a dull green damask cloth dominated the room. Two chairs were placed at either side of an iron cooking range. A sideboard, on which Mole noticed there were framed photographs of what he took to be Charlie as a boy, ran the length of one side of the room, while a low leather settee slept like a large animal on the opposite side containing the window. Here, hunched in a black dress and thick grey shawl, her hands clasped together in her lap, her eyes staring unmovingly into the empty fire grid of the range, sat an old woman—Mrs Stokes—who might, thought Mole, have been a forgotten plaster cast for all the life her body seemed to contain.

"It's Police," said the man, moving round the room to the sideboard and standing with his back to it.

The woman did not look up, but tugged nervously at the shawl, pulling it closer into her neck.

"I . . ." began Mole.

"Don't bother," said the man, fixing his wet eyes on Mole's face. "There's no need. We know what it's about. Don't need to say owt really." His voice trailed away in a long breath and his eyes turned to the woman. "She don't want to hear."

Mole placed his hat on the table and delved for his handkerchief to mop his brow. "I know how you must feel," he began again, then stopped as the woman's face turned to him.

"It were him that that did it!" she hissed, tugging viciously at the shawl. "Him! Alan Tucker!"

"Now gal . . ."

"Mrs Stokes," said Mole. "I . . ."

"*Him*, I say!" Then her face turned away and resumed its vigil of the fire grid.

"Take n'notice, Inspector," said the man. "It's just her way, you know . . . you can see."

"Yes," said Mole, "but perhaps . . ."

"No good going over it all again," the man mumbled as though unaware now of Mole's presence and sinking into a glazed reverie. "Everyone knew on it. He never did get on wi' Charlie, never did, not since a little 'un. Worked for Tucker once, you know, but he always had a down on him Tucker did, all his life. Always finding something to blame him for . . . wanted him out of the way, he did, always. Never said as much, o' course, but he did, you could tell. Now he's done it! He'll be happier like as not. The devil!"

"Devil!" repeated the woman.

"Aye, he's that," droned the man. "He's that and more! Course," his eyes darted to Mole's face, "our Charlie were at a disadvantage, you see. You got to see that first. Him being a bit dim like . . . not very clever, you know, but not simple mark you. No, not that. Very good wi' his hands were Charlie. And sharp — aye, very sharp — always noticing things. Not clever, but smart. *He* didn't like that, Tucker didn't. You could tell. Always reckoned as how Charlie were spying on him. I ask you, spying! What the hell's that when it's about!"

He moved across the room to the woman and placed a hand on her shoulder. "Didn't like our Charlie being about at night, he didn't. But Charlie liked the dark, didn't he, gal? Loved it. Now he's got it alright! He's bloody got it now!"

The man shuddered and the old woman covered his hand with her own. "*Alan Tucker!*" she hissed. "Devil!"

"Charlie knew all about him alright!" choked the man. "He knew . . . he'd seen him, you can bet. You can bloody bet on that, Inspector!"

"Devil!" they murmured together.

And then only their gentle, child-like sobbing filled the room.

# SIXTEEN

There came a time when despair bred more than
heartbreak. It festered into fear and then erupted,
thought Mole as he reached the shade of the wind-break
pines, like a volcano, smearing the venom of its pent up
hate regardless of those it engulfed. Was it ever
justified; did it make sense, or was it simply emotion
running wild? Did the Stokes really believe that Alan
Tucker was responsible for Charlie's death, that in
pursuit of satisfaction for some past disagreement he
had deliberately set out to murder Charlie? Or were
they so caught up in the despair of their loss that only
blind hate had any meaning for them — a straw to clutch
at in bereavement?

In spite of the heat, even here in the shade of the
pines, Mole was aware of a chill along his spine. He had
walked as though in a deep haze of bewilderment and
disbelief from the cottage and along the road towards
Fosbrick, quite oblivious of the fact that he was going
away from Cheal End. He stopped, turned and looked
back to the cluster of buildings. A frown deepened the
creases of his forehead until his eyebrows were pulled
together in a tight, dark line. Somewhere there. . .

"Can I give you a lift, Inspector?"

Mole had neither seen nor heard the Mini slowing to a
halt on the other side of the road. He relaxed the frown,
letting his thoughts escape him, and stared at the
driver.

"Doctor Hill. Sorry, I didn't recognise you."

"You were deep in thought," she said, smiling then

84

climbing out of the car and joining him. "This heat!" She took the loose collars of her open-neck blouse in her hands and wafted them at her neck. "I think it's getting hotter!"

Mole stared at her. The last time they had met she had been as shapeless as a wet sack in her gardening clothes. Now, she was dressed for duty in thin lemon blouse, black skirt and neat sling-back shoes — a transformation that left him staring in admiration for another half-minute.

"Yes," he said at last. "Yes, I think you're right."

"I suppose you've been to the Stokes' home," she said hesitantly. "The whole village is in a state of shock. How are they?"

"Very emotional — as you'd imagine."

"Any help to you?"

Mole took her arm and led her deeper into the wind-break shade.

"I don't honestly know," he said, stopping and turning to face her.

She waited a moment. Then, as though summoning up the confidence to make a confession, said: "Did they tell you about Charlie and Alan Tucker? Do they think he killed Charlie?"

"Yes," said Mole slowly, "very much so. Do you?"

The suddenness of his question dropped like a weight on her breath, forcing her into a startled sigh.

"I . . ." she began.

"Sorry," said Mole, "that was unfair."

"Very," she said, relaxing again.

"Is it common talk — this conflict?"

"I think so."

"Can you tell me about it?" Mole peered anxiously at her, almost willing her to agree that she could and would.

She walked a few paces away from him and leaned on a tree. "Now?" she asked.

"Now if possible," said Mole.

She looked across the fields beyond the wind-break and then back to Mole. Now her eyes were steady, colder.

"It may be all gossip, you know," she began.

"But you don't think so?" Mole prompted.

"I don't know — I just don't know."

"Then tell me what you can" said Mole, his eyes never leaving her face, but remaining calm in their fixed stare.

"Why me?"

"I think you'd put it more fairly than most."

She half smiled. "Thank you. But I've really not been here long enough . . ."

"But you are a doctor," Mole interrupted. "You can make an assessment, and I think you understand people."

She gazed intently at him, searching now for some motive he had not mentioned. "Tell me something first, Inspector. Did whoever killed Marcia also murder Charlie Stokes?"

"It's very likely."

"I see." She paused, eyeing Mole carefully. "Shouldn't you really be talking to Alan Tucker about Charlie?"

"Eventually," said Mole flatly.

"In other words, you want to sound out your ground with me before going into the lion's den?"

"If you like — yes."

"At least you're honest," she said. "Alright, I'll tell you what I've heard, but then you must find out for yourself."

"Thank you," said Mole.

She eased herself away from the tree and walked a few paces deeper into the shade. Turning back to Mole, who had not moved, she said: "I think it's possible — just possible — that the Stokes could be right."

"Why?" asked Mole without a trace of surprise.

"Because I think it very likely that Alan Tucker is not entirely the man most people think him to be." She hesitated, but Mole remained silent, waiting. "No one ever is, of course, I realise that. We all have something that lurks within, escaping every so often to haunt us. But with Alan Tucker it might just be different, or perhaps more positive. I'm not sure." She looked questioningly at Mole, seeking a response.

"Go on," he said quietly.

"Well, the local gossip is that his marriage has never been that successful, although you'd wonder why when you think of Helen Tucker. But there we are, such things happen. Anyway, that's the story, and the trimmings to it are just as you'd imagine—that there have been other women at fairly regular intervals. Nothing lasting or serious, but other women nonetheless. Alan, of course, rides out each storm of talk as though it were all a laugh. He's a very capable man, not easily swayed from a course of action. Blackstock is proof of that."

Mole nodded, his eyes still firmly on Jeanne Hill's face.

"Whether or not there's any real truth in what is said, I have no idea—and I don't think I'm particularly interested. But in a place like Cheal End you learn to live with gossip and whatever happens to be the tale of the day—moreso when you happen to be the local doctor! Everyone seems to think that I should know and add words of wisdom in guidance or something!" She shrugged. "But I was more concerned, I admit, with the recent story Charlie was telling."

"Story?" asked Mole.

"Story—at the moment, because that's what it is as far as I'm concerned. He claimed, not to me personally, but certainly to others, that Alan had . . ." Her eyes widened slightly. "Well, had been having an affair with

Marcia Tucker."

Mole sighed, looked away for a moment, and delved for his handkerchief to mop his brow. "Please go on."

"I can't offer anything very tangible, but the story is that soon after John Tucker's death Charlie Stokes went to work for Marcia. He never had employment for very long, which is understandable. Mostly odd jobbing work around the village. However, Marcia was grateful for any help, even the efforts of Charlie. He hadn't been at the farm long before he—so he said—found them, Alan and Marcia, well, together. Apparently it went on for some weeks."

She stopped, looked away again and scuffed a shoe in the dried undergrowth. "It's an even bet, Inspector," she said, a sudden sarcasm in her voice, "an even bet either way. Charlie may have been romanticizing, or he may have been telling the truth."

"What do you think?" said Mole.

"Me?" She was startled. "I don't think my opinions really count! But if you want one, I think it's easy—very easy—to put Marcia into almost any category of depravity you care to choose. She's dead now. She wasn't wanted while she lived. Does it matter!"

She shivered in sudden anger, glared at Mole, then snapped: "Oh, what the hell!" And ran from the shade to the car.

"Doctor Hill!" Mole moved to follow her, but was too late. The car pulled away in a violent thrust of power and was gone.

"Damn!" croaked Mole to himself and turned to see Sergeant Fisher easing his sweating bulk from the Hillman parked further along the road.

"Ah, sir!" began Fisher, moving now at a gentle but lumbering trot. "Found you!"

"Yes, Sergeant, what is it?" said Mole, the irritation within him clipping his words.

"It's the solicitor—Robins. He's missing, sir."

"Missing! What do you mean, missing?"

"Just that, sir. No one — not his office, his home — no one has seen him since last Friday."

"Damn!" said Mole again.

"But I think we may have an idea where he is, sir," said Fisher, loosening his collar as he kept pace with Mole towards the waiting car. "He has a boat at Windfleet. He could be there."

"We'll try it," said Mole. "Now! Fast as you can!"

# SEVENTEEN

". . .so when I got back to Moston," said Fisher, his eyes firmly on the road ahead, his foot hard on the Hillman's accelerator, "there was Baxter hopping about like a demented frog, trying to establish where Robins might have gone. He hadn't been seen at his office since last Thursday night—left no message with his partner as to where he was going, and there was nothing in his appointment book. Baxter tried his home—he lives with his Mother—and drew another blank there. She hadn't seen him since Friday morning. Apparently he left home at the usual time soon after nine, his normal self, saying he'd see her later. Anyway . . ."

Mole was annoyed with himself. He should not have let Jeanne Hill go away like that; he should have recognised that she had been too close to Marcia Tucker, felt too deeply for her, to want to talk of what she had heard. He should have been gentler, firmer, or perhaps more realistic.

". . . Baxter probed a bit deeper," said Fisher, swinging the car violently to the right into a narrow lane that skirted the Northern perimeter of Cheal End and headed out towards the estuary at Windfleet. "Seems Robins' Mother had no real idea of what her son might be doing or where he might be. Then she mentioned the boat. He often went there, she said, mostly at week-ends and holidays, but always when he had something on his mind, something to work out, and he had been looking a bit thoughtful lately. So Baxter was just about to set off with half the Force when I arrived . . ."

Jeanne Hill must have known of the story of Alan Tucker when they first talked, thought Mole. But it was, as she had said, a story—a conglomeration of gossip. Why inflict more on Marcia's reputation? Even so, it was important, and Alan Tucker would certainly have some explaining to do. . .

"Yes," said Mole to himself and the road ahead, "that's for sure."

Fisher glanced at him. "What is, sir?"

"Hmmm?" Mole pulled himself away from his thoughts. "Oh, the boat—Robins' boat. That must be it."

"Well, I think there's a very fair chance," said Fisher, forcing the Hillman ahead still faster. "He's probably been there all the time. Hiding out. There's no doubt about it, sir," he went on, a fresh confidence deepening his voice, "he's our man alright. Stands to reason. If he went missing on Friday, he'd have had plenty of time to get rid of Mrs Tucker. As for Charlie Stokes—well, there again, ample time to do the job. And it was a smart move to dump the body back at the dyke at the Crossing—keeping the suspicion local, you see."

Mole did not answer. He simply watched the grey slick of road rushing to meet them and the blue mass of the sky that sat like a smooth, fat and very contented balloon on the flat lands of the oncoming estuary.

Twenty-minutes later, Sergeant Fisher rolled the Hillman to a halt on the dusty track that flanked the moorings at Windfleet, switched off the engine, wound down the window and sat back to mop his sweating brow.

"The bloomin' heat, sir!" he choked. "It's like a furnace!"

Mole stared about him without making any attempt to move. His eyes followed the line of boats lying drunkenly around the inlet at low tide. The mud, baked to a crusty hardness under the fierce sunlight, seemed almost to shimmer in its smoothness. The small rivulets of sea water lay still and thin like slivers of clear glass. There was no movement for as far as the eye could see; no sound save for the lonely call of a curlew somewhere deep in the tinder-brown undergrowth.

"What's the name of the boat?" he asked.

"Reedcutter, sir," said Fisher, replacing his handkerchief. "She's a pleasure craft. Cabin cruiser. Shouldn't be hard to spot. They're mostly fishing vessels down here."

They climbed out of the car and Fisher pointed to a line of boats moored further inland. "Over there, I reckon, sir," he said. "That's where the week-enders have their spot."

"He could have gone to sea," said Mole, setting off along the track.

"Could have, sir, that's true. But I don't think so. I think he'll have stayed put."

Mole grunted. "Not much chance of our arriving unnoticed," he said, as they walked into the flat, table-top landscape. "He'll have spotted us by now."

"And we can spot him if *he* makes a move," said Fisher, quickening his pace ahead of Mole.

They walked on for another five minutes, checking carefully the name of each boat as they passed it. They saw no one, heard nothing. Now even the curlew had ceased to call. All that broke the silence of the still, hot day was the crackle of their footsteps through the stiff grass.

"There, sir!" said Fisher a minute later as the low, sleek line of a white and blue painted hull came into their view, the name *Reedcutter* picked out in heavy gold lettering along the stern. "That's her!" whispered Fisher as both he and Mole stopped, waited and watched.

"There's someone aboard, sir," murmured Fisher, his eyes narrowing. "Look!" He pointed to where a door stood open in the well of the stern deck. Beyond it, they could see the shadowed outline of a figure, half bent over a table, its fingers working quickly through a pile of papers.

"Robins?" said Mole.

"Can't tell from here," said Fisher. "But it must be."

They moved closer, Mole leading now, the muscles tense in the back of his neck, the sweat slipping icily over his back.

Five yards, four, three . . . Mole came up to his full height. "Mr Robins!" he called, as Fisher moved nimbly round to his left to reach the blind side.

The man scattered the papers in his surprise, scrambled from the cabin to the deck, and with one desperate leap reached the track, landing on all-fours at Fisher's feet.

Fisher made a grab at the man's flimsy linen coat, missed, and stumbled headlong down the short slope of the bank into the boat's side.

"Damn!" shouted Fisher, then rolled over in time to see Mole lunging forward like a hunting animal, arms outstretched, fingers clawing at the air and the man's billowing jacket.

Mole pounced, connected first with cloth, then flesh, and finally the bulk of the man, bringing him down in a spinning, gasping heap.

"My god!" said Fisher, grabbing at the man's thrashing legs as Mole hit the ground with a thud that pummelled the breath from his body.

"It's Mark Gerson!"

# EIGHTEEN

"Alright, alright!" snapped Gerson. "You can lay off the rough stuff!" He pulled his right arm from Fisher's grasp, shoved the long black hair from his eyes and struggled to bring back some shape to his twisted, crumpled jacket.

"Watch it!" said Fisher, moving round to place Gerson between himself and Mole.

"No trouble," soothed Gerson, turning to Mole who was brushing the dust from his hat and breathing like a veteran steam engine. "You Inspector Mole?" he asked, sweeping the sweat from his forehead with his jacket sleeve.

"That's right," said Mole. He placed his hat firmly back on his head. "And you're Mark Gerson, and you're in a mess!"

Gerson did not answer. He turned back to Fisher. "Who told you I was here?"

"No one," said Fisher. "We just happened to be out for a quiet stroll!"

Gerson smiled. He was a thin, wiry man, somewhere in his mid-thirties, thought Mole, as he took in the long nose, straggling mouth and small brown eyes—a man who, given the right setting and the benefit of an expensive but not necessarily tasteful wardrobe, would be dubbed a smoothy. He would be the soft-lipped talker with the instant smile that flattered silly girls—and promptly landed them in bed at the promise of a bauble or two. Mole winced—at the pain in his shoulders and at the sight of the sweating jeweller. He liked neither.

"There's a perfectly simple explanation for all this," said Gerson, adjusting his trousers then fidgeting with his collar and tie.

"I'm sure," said Mole irritably. "Suppose you begin at the beginning, Mr Gerson — just for our benefit!"

Gerson's smile faded. The sweat on his face had turned colder, flattening to a grimy pack of dust. He ran his fingers over it, darkening the patches round his eyes and smearing his cheeks with grey streaks.

"Alright," he said, thrusting back his shoulders. "I'm game for that, Inspector."

"You haven't much choice," said Mole. "Now get on with it!"

"Come on," added Fisher, giving him a gentle nudge on the shoulder. "What were you doing aboard that boat — you know it belongs to Steven Robins? And where's he, as a matter of interest?"

"One thing at a time!" said Gerson, twitching his shoulder out of Fisher's reach. "I don't know where Steven Robins is. That's why I'm here."

"Breaking and entering," said Fisher.

"Not on your life!" mocked Gerson, taking a key from his trousers pocket and dangling it in Fisher's face. "*This* fits *that* cabin and Robins knows I have it. I was here simply to get back what is rightfully mine."

"Oh, and what would that be, Mr Gerson?" asked Mole.

"Money," said Gerson. "Plain, ordinary money — which Robins owes me, which he won't pay, which he says he hasn't got, and which he won't even talk about. He gave me the key to the boat as a sort of insurance — just in case he couldn't pay up. I was down here to see if . . ."

"Money for what?"

"For fancy gifts for his fancy woman!" Gerson's lips curled in a sneer.

"And who might that be?"

"Was, Inspector, was. Marcia Tucker, of course."

Mole looked quickly at Fisher, then back to Gerson.
"He told you that?"

"He didn't have to tell me, Inspector. I bloody well
introduced them! She was my . . ." he hesitated, his
glare darting from Mole to Fisher then to Mole again.
"My friend until a few months ago, then Robins took
over. Bloody fool! I warned him — but, oh no, clever
little Steven wouldn't be told!"

"You're not making much sense, Mr Gerson," said
Mole quietly. "Let's take it a step at a time, shall we,
from the beginning.

Gerson sighed, pulled at his collar, and shrugged.
"Okay," he said, "from the beginning. I took up with
Marcia Tucker soon after her husband died. She hit the
town, Inspector — a big spender — nice clothes, nice
jewellery, whatever took her fancy. And that included
men, although she wasn't too particular about them!"
He shrugged again and sniffed. "Anyway, I met her
through my shop as much as anything. You should have
seen the way she spent — like it was water! Not that I
minded, of course. I mean, business is business when
all's said and paid for!" He smiled, received no response
from either Mole or Fisher, and went on: "So there we
were, thrust together you might say. And she was good
fun — a bit flighty, I'll grant you, but it made life
interesting. And . . ." He held up a hand as though in
justification. "I make no bones about it, I do like my
women to be just a shade unpredictable! Keeps you
active, if you follow me!" Again he looked to Mole and
Fisher. Again he met blank stares. "Alright, so I admit
it — I was taking her for what I could get, and so long as
the money held out and the spending kept up, I was
happy. And so was she."

"And Steven Robins," said Mole, "when did he enter
this happy fold?"

Gerson disregarded Mole's cynicism. "To name a date, that I couldn't do. But I reckon we'd been knocking about for perhaps a month—maybe more—when I introduced her to Robins at The George. They took to each other like fish to a pond—which is what they were, in a way: two fish swimming about, neither of them sure of where they were going. Ah, but then perhaps you don't know our Mr Robins that well, Inspector?"

"Not that well at all," said Mole.

"Well, he's one on his own. Very clever, brilliant in fact, but a real loner. Lives with his Mum, you know, and never so much as looked at a woman. But I digress . . ."

Gerson swelled with renewed confidence as he warmed to his tale. He fumbled in his jacket pockets for cigarettes and a lighter, offered them, was refused, and puffed quietly for a moment before continuing.

"It was obvious that Robins and Marcia were going to make something big of each other. Don't ask me why, but I could sense it. They gelled, you know—really got the chemistry mixing. So that's when I dropped out of the scene. I mean, I don't share my women with anyone! And in any case, I'd no need to worry; the spending kept up, except that this time it was Steven Robins who was doing it all for her. Couldn't lavish enough on her—rings, brooches, pearls, anything that took her eye. Of course, her taste wasn't always that good—a bit cheap and gaudy sometimes—but who was I to query a quid or so when it was regular?"

Mole glanced at Fisher whose face looked just how Mole felt: sick and sorry.

"But then that's when things got a shade difficult," said Gerson, slowing the tempo of his voice. "Robins started to take things on credit—not that I minded at first, you understand. Good custom needs a bit of leeway here and there. But I did get worried when he reached three-hundred and not a penny paid back."

"That's what he owes you?" said Mole.

"Nearer five-hundred now."

"You approached him about the amount?" asked Mole in the most unemotional tone he could muster.

"*Approached* him! I practically threatened murder . . ." Gerson swallowed on the word, a white panic sliding across his face. "Well, not in so many words, of course. What I mean to say is that, well, I made it perfectly clear that I couldn't stand that sort of outstanding debt. After all, business is . . ."

"Quite," interrupted Mole. "Then what?"

"He said he needed time. Funds were a bit low, that sort of thing. Oh, I've heard it all before, believe me! Still, he was my solicitor. We were scratching each other's backs, sort of, so I was prepared to wait—for so long."

"When did he tell you he was going to marry Marcia?" said Mole with a suddenness that stiffened Gerson's back and brought a low cough from Fisher.

Gerson threw down his cigarette and ground it out with a slow, steady motion of his right foot. When he looked back to Mole, his eyes had darkened as though a cloud had passed miraculously over the blazing sun.

"Not many know about that," he said slowly.

"I do," said Mole.

"Guesswork, Inspector, or fact?"

It was Mole's turn to stiffen.

"Calculated guesswork, I'd say," said Gerson, his stare as fixed as cold stone. "But you're right, he was planning something of the sort. And I say *of the sort* advisedly, because I know for a fact he never intended going through with it!"

## NINETEEN

Mole blinked into the sunlight and tasted the saltiness of his own sweat as it trickled into the corners of his mouth. He swallowed. "For a fact, Mr Gerson?" he croaked, eyeing the bulk of Fisher in what now seemed to be a shimmering haze of heat.

"For a fact, Inspector," said Gerson, fumbling for another cigarette, then changing his mind. "I warned him Marcia was unpredictable long before he got going with her—and expensive. And he found that out for sure! She dropped him in a real financial mess, but that still didn't put him off wanting to marry her—not at first, anyway. He told me about it, of course, and I let him have my opinion in no uncertain terms. I told him he was a fool to even think of it. She wasn't ready for another marriage and there was too much at stake for him professionally. He'd have to leave Moston for sure—and so on and so on. A dozen and more things were against it. But no, he wouldn't listen. He said they'd sell the farm and move to London. He'd had a good offer there and it was time, anyway, he got out of the Fens."

"So what put him off?" said Fisher.

Gerson hesitated. Again he thought about a cigarette, made the movements to light one, but held it unlit between his fingers.

"Two things. First, he found out about Marcia's association with Henry Layton, which you may or may not know about, Inspector. He didn't like that, but somehow or other it was all smoothed over. Anyway,

Layton was an old man and she wasn't likely to go setting up home with him. But there was something else—and that did it."

Now Gerson lit the cigarette and relished the smoke. Mole waited, Fisher shifted from one foot to the other. Above them, the sun beat down relentlessly.

"God knows how, but he came to hear that Marcia had been having a high old time with her brother-in-law, Alan Tucker, the one man she'd always reckoned was at the root of her troubles." Gerson inhaled deeply on the cigarette. "As I say, I don't know how he came to find out about the affair—and I don't know if there's an ounce of truth in it—but somehow, from someone, he did."

"Did he say anything to Mrs Tucker?" asked Mole.

"No, he didn't," said Gerson, "and that's what I couldn't understand. He told me, but said he wouldn't say anything to her until he was absolutely sure."

"When was this?"

"About a fortnight ago."

"And?"

"Oh, he established that there'd been something going on right enough," said Gerson, "no doubt about that. I saw him last Wednesday night at The George in Moston, and he said he knew everything. But he wouldn't say how he'd found out or who'd told him."

"Do you know where Robins is now?" said Fisher.

"No clues here," said Gerson, nodding to the boat. "The only place I can think of—unless he's out of the country, of course—is the Saracen's Head at Swinesleigh. He sometimes stayed there at week-ends."

"When Robins told you of having established the fact of Mrs Tucker's affair with her brother-in-law, did he say anything else?" said Mole.

"He went white with—with hate, anger, I don't know. He said . . ." Gerson cleared the sweat from his forehead with the back of his hand. "He said he'd see her in hell!"

The sun blazed on. . .

## TWENTY

"You're frowning and you're pacing, Arthur, and I know the signs," said Superintendent Hayes from behind his clear, clean and highly polished desk at Police headquarters in Moston. "Either you're very close, or you're very troubled. Which is it?"

Mole reached the window of the second floor office and stared into the empty street below. The sun had finally given up for the day and settled in a splash of vivid colours in the West. But the air was still heavy and thick like an invisible drape drawn across the land, so that each movement of the body became a determined effort — and after the sort of day he'd had, one of sheer endurance. He half smiled to himself, turned and walked back into the room.

"I could be close, I could be troubled. I know I'm hot and I know I'm tired — and I wish to heaven Fisher would call in from Swinesleigh!"

"He will," said Hayes. "Give him time."

"Should have gone with him," said Mole in a low mutter.

"On what could well prove a wild-goose chase? No, Arthur, you're better employed here at the moment." Hayes leaned back in his chair. "Why don't you sit down?"

"I prefer to walk," said Mole, and set off for the window again.

"Do you think they'll find Robins at Swinesleigh?"

asked Hayes.

"I believe so," said Mole, staring into the explosive sky. "If they don't, we're sunk. It'll be out of our territory and a Yard job."

"Then Robins is our man?"

Mole waited a moment before answering. "Could be. But we shan't know until we've heard his side of the story. And then again . . ."

"Oh, come on, Arthur," interrupted Hayes. "What's *really* troubling you?"

Mole sighed. "If I could put that in a nutshell, I'd be a happy man. But I can't. All I do know is that something — something, somewhere — is not fitting the pattern."

"Alan Tucker?"

"Hmmm," droned Mole thoughtfully. "I don't know about him."

"I think I do," said Hayes, leaning forward again. "I think we've dragged a few skeletons out of Mr Tucker's cupboard. You're rattling the bones, Arthur — and I'm damn sure he isn't going to like it!"

"Hmmm," droned Mole again. "He could have murdered Mrs Tucker — but then there's the alibi."

"Sound?"

"Too sound," said Mole. "Too neat, too careful, too ready-made for the job."

"You'll see him again?"

"Tonight," said Mole, walking back to the window. "As soon as Fisher calls in, I'm off to Cheal End — whatever the time."

"And if Fisher's bringing Robins in?"

"I want Robins to cool off here for a while — give him time to realise that he's in our hands now and had better start telling his story in very careful detail."

"It's your case, Arthur," said Hayes, coming to his feet. "Fancy a drink?"

"Not really," said Mole. "I'll wait till I'm home."

Hayes walked slowly to the window, head down, steps measured, hands in pockets. "What about Gerson?"

"We couldn't hold him," said Mole grudgingly. "He had the key to the boat and as far as we're concerned wasn't doing anything criminal. Robins had unwittingly given him every right to be there. A pity."

"A nasty character," scowled Hayes.

"Very. But useful. He probably knows more about Marcia Tucker than most."

"Could he have killed her is more to the point?"

"We took a statement from him when we got back here. Apparently he left his shop at four-fifteen on that Friday to deliver some jewellery to a client at The George and stayed for a few drinks and a chat, as he put it, until well after five-thirty. I've had that checked and it holds up."

"What about the night of Charlie Stokes' death?"

"Watertight alibi!" said Mole with a hint of sarcasm. "He was in his flat all night with a certain Miss Ruby Lysaght—who has a very new and very expensive bracelet to prove it, according to Baxter! No, sir, he's in the clear there."

"Meanwhile, he goes free?"

"He won't run, if that's what you're thinking," said Mole. "He'll be around—waiting for his money!"

Hayes walked back to his desk. He gazed down at the polished top for a moment, then said: "Whoever killed Mrs Tucker also murdered Charlie—that must be so, mustn't it, Arthur?"

"At least I'm sure of that," said Mole, "although the time of death leaves the field wide open. Baxter's collecting statements, but it's my guess we'll find most people were indoors either sleeping, or, like Gerson, otherwise engaged."

Hayes sat down. "What about Henry Layton and the blackmail letter? Any ideas on that?"

"Sent by the murderer. It was part of his plan to set

the hares running in all directions—particularly Fisher and me—and it worked! We know now that Gerson knew of Layton's association with Mrs Tucker, and if what he says is true, so did Robins. And perhaps Alan Tucker knew of it."

"But we rule out Layton as a suspect?"

"Not necessarily. He could have sent the letter to himself. He could have made the trip to Cheal End on the Friday even though he'd have to have driven like hell to get there after waiting until four-o'clock to meet the horse buyer—who didn't turn up, by the way. We've established that."

Hayes frowned. "And Robins?"

"Ah!" said Mole, setting off from the window at a livelier pace. "Now there we have the totally unknown."

"Why associate with the woman in the first place—that's what beats me. I mean, he's a solicitor—a brilliant one too, I'm told—and she was, well, little more than a whore. Where's the sense and logic in that? Or am I being very naive?"

"A bit naive, sir," said Mole through a suppressed smile. "But there are two possible answers. One, Steven Robins liked the idea of marrying Moston's whore. Two, Marcia Tucker wasn't all whore."

"But he must have known of her reputation. There was Layton—Gerson says he knew about him and of the affair with Alan Tucker. Was it that discovery that finally put him off marriage?"

Mole rubbed his chin. "Gerson certainly thinks so. But who told Robins about her affair with Tucker? Not Tucker, I'm sure!"

"Charlie Stokes!" smiled Hayes triumphantly.

"Perhaps."

"In which case," Hayes rushed on, "Charlie would know that Robins was a likely murderer—and hey presto!"

"On the other hand . . ." began Mole.

Hayes lifted a hand as the telephone on his desk gave a tight shrill.

"Hayes," he said, taking the receiver, his eyes on Mole's face. "Very good. Yes, I see. Good. Excellent. Thank you, Sergeant." He replaced the receiver.

"There you are, Arthur," he said smiling. "That was Fisher. They've got Robins, no trouble. He was, as we thought, at the Saracen's Head and has been since Friday, or so he says. Fisher's bringing him in now."

"Did Fisher say . . ."

"He said that all Robins had done so far was to remain absolutely silent, but co-operative. Well, after all, he is a solicitor!"

Mole smiled. "Preparing his own brief!"

"Naturally!"

Minutes later, Mole climbed into the Hillman and turned the nose for Cheal End.

The evening dusk had already deepened into night as he drove alongside the dyke towards the Cheal Crossing then slowed at the turning for the bridge, glanced down at the spot where Marcia Tucker had lain, and for a moment was quite certain that the smell of death wafted in through the car's open windows.

He accelerated in the direction of Blackstock.

## TWENTY-ONE

It was a lonely room — long, low-ceilinged and strangely remote from all that Mole had come to regard as the highly charged and sophisticated atmosphere of Blackstock.

He found it hard to believe that this room, with its tightness, brusque and almost fierce furniture, inadequate lighting and old and faded early watercolours of Fenland scenes, was a part of the Tucker's life. What was it, he wondered as he gazed round, that could create in space a sense of loss and foreboding, as though inhabited by the ghosts and voices of past years? And where was the panache of the study he had seen yesterday? There was no assurance here, thought Mole, only the lurking shadows of figures that had flitted through, out of time and reality, leaving nothing behind but their loneliness.

Or was this the reality? Was this the real life of the Tuckers and Blackstock — dark and unconnected like a still night without stars or sounds?

He waited a moment, heard Alan Tucker close the front door, then walked over to the window where the curtains remained open and the darkness seemed to seep in over the sill. He turned as Tucker entered the room, a surprised and questioning look on his face, his eyes keen and incredibly blue in the half light.

"Now, Inspector," he said, allowing a faint smile to cross his lips, "this is a surprise. I hadn't thought we'd meet again quite so soon. There must be something I can help with. Will you have a drink?" Tucker moved towards a heavy sideboard on which was arranged a selection of bottles and glasses. He helped himself to a Scotch without waiting for Mole's answer.

"No thank you, sir," said Mole, walking slowly from the window to the table, placing his hat on it, and unbuttoning his jacket. "I'm sorry to bother you at this time, and without letting you know I was on my way."

"Think nothing of it, Inspector, although you're lucky to find me in. I'm supposed to be attending a village Community Centre meeting with my wife tonight, but to be frank I couldn't bear the thought of it! So here I am. Now, what can I do for you?"

"Well, this won't take long if you still want to make the meeting," said Mole, his eyes firmly on Tucker's face.

"Oh, no chance of that, Inspector!"

"Then in that case . . ."

"Look," said Tucker, moving closer and at the same time taking a large gulp of his drink, "before you tell me what it is I can help with, I must say . . . well, I want to say how sorry I am about Charlie. It really is a tragedy, Inspector. Heaven knows, I've lived here all my life, but never have I felt such an air of hate and mistrust. It's like a nightmare. As I was saying to your man Baxter this afternoon, when the devil is it going to end?"

"Oh, it'll end," said Mole calmly, "you can be quite sure of that." He paused. "I take it you gave Baxter an account of where you were at the time Charlie Stokes was killed?"

"Yes, of course," said Tucker, staring into the drink. "My wife and I dined together, had a few drinks while watching television, and went to bed about nine-thirtyish." He smiled lightly. "As far as I'm concerned, I didn't stir again until six."

"I appreciate your assisting Baxter, sir," said Mole, sliding a hand into his jacket pocket. "With another murder on our hands, we're having to go over the ground again, so to speak. But it is about Charlie Stokes that I wanted to see you. I understand you had known him all your life and that he once worked for you?"

Tucker finished his drink hurriedly, placed the glass on the table, walked over to the fireplace and stood with his back to it.

"Yes, Inspector, I'd known Charlie since I was a boy. We grew up together almost. I suppose . . ." Tucker hesitated. "I suppose you know he was not . . . well, not quite normal?"

Mole made no attempt to comment.

"Not quite the village idiot," said Tucker, "but close enough. It was a great shame. Amos and his wife took it very badly, Charlie being their only child. However, as in most cases of this type, the village rallied in support. Amos was never without work, and Charlie worked here. But unfortunately . . ." He hesitated again, this time taking his eyes from Mole and turning his stare to the window. "Unfortunately, I had to ask him to leave."

"Why was that, sir?"

Tucker sighed. "Well, to be frank, Inspector, he had a most annoying habit of watching my wife. No, that doesn't sound quite right put like that. He—well, he was always hovering around her and she was never certain when or where he'd appear next. I tried to reassure her that Charlie was harmless enough, but I'm afraid the matter got worse until one day I found him here, in the house, in our bedroom. And, well, there was nothing I could do. He had to go."

"I see, sir," said Mole. "What happened then?"

"I'm afraid he didn't take it very kindly, nor did his parents. In fact, they waged something of a war on both myself and my wife—and Blackstock, come to that. You know the sort of thing—malicious gossip, wild stories. I took little notice of them, but I'm not so sure others turned such a deaf ear."

"You mean they believed him?"

"Not exactly. But that sort of talk is quite enough to set tongues wagging out of all proportion, Inspector, as you well know."

"What sort of gossip was Charlie putting about, sir?" asked Mole.

The brightness in Tucker's eyes faded and a grey, pinched look settled on his face.

"I'd rather not discuss that, Inspector, if you don't mind."

"As you wish, sir," said Mole. "But I wouldn't want to get the wrong impression."

Tucker's eyes narrowed. "Very well. He seemed to be convinced that I was leading a double life. That I had *lady friends*, as he put it, and that I was far from faithful to my wife."

"Hmmm," said Mole, moving to the window and gazing out into the night.

"Naturally, it was all lies," said Tucker to his back.

Mole waited a moment, then turned gently but deliberately to face him. "Can you recall exactly when Charlie went to work for Marcia Tucker?"

Alan Tucker's hands tightened in an almost imperceptible clench and he gazed at Mole in a long, unblinking stare. Slowly, as though marking the intensity of his thoughts, a frown began above his eyes, knotting the skin into dark hummocks. His lips moved apart, but he made no sound.

"He did work for her?" said Mole, the question sharpened to break both the silence and Alan Tucker's concentration.

"Yes—yes, he did." Tucker's frown broke, the hummocks relaxed as he marshalled his thoughts. "And that would be—oh, let me see," Tucker went on easily, turning his eyes to the ceiling, "well, shortly after my brother's death."

"How long was he there?"

"Two months or so—no more."

"Do you know why he left, sir?"

"No," said Tucker, "except that . . ."

"It wouldn't have been because of anything you did or said, would it?"

"I'm not sure I follow you, Inspector."

Mole kept his gaze steady, his hands flat now on the table, his body leaning forward.

"There's some talk that you and your sister-in-law were having an affair and that Charlie knew of it."

Tucker did not flinch. The blueness of his eyes turned colder, but there was neither movement nor expression to hint at any surprise. "Talk you say. Well, that's what it is, Inspector — talk. And originated, I've no doubt, by Charlie Stokes."

"No doubt," said Mole, "but what I'm interested in is whether or not there's any truth in it."

"You believe it?"

"I didn't say so — but if it is true, then it may well alter my thinking about some aspects of this case, and it certainly puts you, sir, in a new light."

"It makes it highly likely that I killed Marcia — and possibly Charlie?"

"It may give you a motive for murder, but not necessarily make you a murderer. What it could mean is that you were a good deal closer to your sister-in-law than I have been led to believe, and that leaves me wondering . . ."

"Leaves you wondering why," interrupted Tucker.

"Exactly."

They stared at each other intently.

"Well, sir, was there an affair?" said Mole a shade more irritably than he had intended.

The room had grown warmer and stickier with the night heat. Mole wanted desperately to fling open the windows and let what little cool air there was across the Fens drift in and over him. So, perhaps, did Alan Tucker, but he showed no signs of either discomfort or concern.

"If you mean were we going to bed—no, we weren't. But there was a closeness, something that developed over the weeks. She certainly became more affectionate—and often showed it. But then I heard of the sort of life she was leading in Moston and . . ." Tucker's face tightened. "It was obvious what she was becoming, so I decided to make my move for the farm."

"You offered to buy it?"

"Yes. And she just laughed at me. She would have none of it, as you know."

Mole reached for his hat.

"Did Charlie Stokes see anything at all that could have made him think there was an affair going on between yourself and Mrs Tucker?"

"Oh, he must have seen *something*, Inspector—a quick hug, something equally innocent. Anything, in fact. But knowing Charlie, he would quite easily construe that as the grand illicit passion! He had that sort of mind."

Mole turned his hat in his hands, staring thoughtfully at the revolving rim.

"Are you aware that your sister-in-law planned to marry again?" he said, his eyes moving quickly to Tucker's face.

"My wife told me of that this afternoon, and it's ridiculous!" scoffed Tucker. "I don't believe a word of it, Inspector! Who'd want to marry her, anyway?"

"Steven Robins," said Mole quietly.

"The solicitor? Rubbish! Not in a million years! No, you're way out there, Inspector—way out!"

"Oh, and why's that, sir?"

"Because it's my belief that Marcia had already agreed to let Mark Gerson sell the farm. He, after all, was the only man who had any real influence over her."

"Gerson?" said Mole more to himself than to Tucker. "You know Mark Gerson?"

"Very well. He's what used years ago, Inspector, to be known as a scoundrel. A lousy reputation with women—and a highly suspect one in business!" There was a viciousness in Tucker's tone and a recharged glint in his eyes.

"What sort of an influence did he have over your sister-in-law!"

"A purely monetary one to begin with, I suspect, due to her irrational tastes and indulgence in jewellery. But she was fascinated by him—couldn't leave him alone. The outcome, of course, was inevitable." He paused. "I happen to know, Inspector, that Mark Gerson was lining up a buyer for the farm."

"How do you *happen* to know, sir?"

"Because Gerson told me!"

Mole could feel a cold sweat breaking out in the nape of his neck. "When was this, sir?" he asked calmly.

"Oh, a few weeks ago. I forget precisely when. I met him—or at least he joined me—at the bar in The George one lunchtime. Said I might be interested to hear that he'd found a buyer for the Tucker farm—acting, as he put it, on Marcia's instructions." Tucker paused, but met only a straight stare from Mole. "I wished him well, but warned him that he'd have me to contend with in any selling arrangement. I said I'd have a word with Marcia as soon as I could—to which he smiled in that supercilious way of his, and left."

"Did you speak to her?"

"No, I tried to contact Marcia on two or three occasions, but she was always out. I decided in the end to leave the matter, having warned my solicitors to keep an ear to the ground."

"You thought Gerson was bluffing?"

"Not a bit, Inspector! He was sincere enough. The question is—was Marcia?"

## TWENTY-TWO

Mark Gerson! The name thudded at the back of Mole's head like the long roll of thunder he wished would herald the break in the freak November weather. Could it really be that Gerson, after all and in spite of his alibis, was the single element that had controlled the life and death of Marcia Tucker — and that of Charlie Stokes?

Was it possible that his explanation of his own affair with her and the relationship he had described between Robins and Marcia, were no more than a concocted series of deceits to cover the real depth of his own closeness and influence over her? And had that influence finally extended to forcing Marcia to sell the farm to a buyer of his choice — with no doubt suitable interest payable to himself? Would Marcia have gone along with such a scheme; had she refused — or had she, as Tucker had suggested, called his bluff?

Mole slowed the Hillman to a halt a yard or so beyond the Stone Cottages in Cheal End and relaxed in his seat. He knew he should be driving fast for Moston and the meeting with Steven Robins. Instead, he had turned left out of Blackstock, the slim silhouette of Alan Tucker waving nonchalantly to him from the doorway of the farm house, and cruised almost aimlessly towards the cluster of cottage lights in the distance.

He parked opposite the Five Cats from which now, through the open windows, there came the steady hum of customers' conversation and the lazy curl of soft blue smoke. A pint of beer, he thought, would be as welcome as a cool breeze, but he turned his eyes away from the inviting glow of the lounge bar and stared ahead into the darkness of the Fenland night, his thoughts twisting back to Blackstock, the stifling room and the enigmatic gaze of Alan Tucker.

Slowly, as his reverie eased and he was conscious again of his surroundings, his fingers slid to the ignition key, then paused as he became aware of a figure hurrying towards him. It was Helen Tucker. She was about to cross to the other side of the road as Mole wound down the passenger seat window and called to her.

"Can I give you a lift, Mrs Tucker?"

She stopped, turned and peered into the darkness of the car, then approached it gingerly.

"Hope I didn't startle you," said Mole as she reached the open window and stared at him.

"Oh, it's you, Inspector," she said with a quick smile of recognition. "You're the last person I expected to meet tonight. Are you going my way?"

"I'm about to head back to Moston. It'd be no trouble to drop you at Blackstock."

"Thank you." She climbed into the car and slammed the door shut. "I've just been to one of those interminably long meetings at which nothing is ever resolved!"

"I know them well!" Mole slipped the car into gear and headed slowly back towards Blackstock.

"Not that I'm surprised, really. The village is in such a state of shock. All anyone can talk about is . . ."

She chatted amiably on, but Mole had already noticed that she looked pale and withdrawn as though in slow conflict with a problem whose resolve she still could not see.

Her eyes had lost the gleam of vitality which had so fascinated him on their first meeting. Now they were flat and sunken under the strain of preoccupation. Her

114

face, no longer that of the softly sculptured figurine, was tight and anxious, the flesh drawn back in dark patches over the small bones.

Mole waited until she had finished her account of the talk at the meeting, then said: "As a matter of fact, I've just come from Blackstock."

"I guessed as much," she said without looking at Mole. "I suppose you've been discussing Charlie Stokes with Alan." She stared straight ahead, following the probe of the headlights on the grey road.

"You knew I would?"

"I knew you'd hear the rumours and gossip sooner or later. And I could imagine what you'd deduce from them."

"I'm not sure I've deduced anything, Mrs Tucker."

She smiled wryly and turned to look at him.

"You don't have to be kind, Inspector. I've known Alan a long time." She paused, her gaze steady but suddenly very lonely. "And I've lived in Cheal End a long time—perhaps too long. I'm very well aware of what is being said."

Mole was in no hurry to answer. He glanced quickly at her face, noting the firmer line to her mouth and the merest hint of new life in her eyes.

"Perhaps you can tell me if there's any truth in what I've been hearing?" he said, slowing down as they approached the drive to Blackstock, then stopping at the entrance.

Now Helen Tucker's eyes widened and settled calmly but thoughtfully on Mole's face. For all the warmth of the night, she hugged the open cardigan draped across her shoulders.

"It would be ridiculous to suggest that the stories are all lies. You wouldn't believe me, anyway." She looked away again, not waiting for an answer. "In any case, I'm sure Alan's made the position quite clear."

Suddenly, there was the snap of defiance in her voice.

"I'm not sure where all the rumour places your sister-in-law," said Mole. "I'm being asked to believe a lot of the reputation of Marcia Tucker. Far more, I think, than is really the case." He paused. "We may have found the man she was going to marry, by the way."

Helen Tucker's head turned slowly to face Mole, but there was neither surprise nor agitation in her expression. "Who?" was all she asked coldly.

"We think her solicitor, Steven Robins. He's in Moston at the moment, helping with inquiries."

"Very likely she was," said Helen Tucker in an almost off-hand, disinterested manner.

"You don't sound surprised."

"I don't know the man, Inspector. As far as I'm concerned, she could have been marrying the man-in-the-moon. She never discussed it with me. The first I heard of the marriage was after our meeting in Blatley's, as I've already told you."

"Your husband seems to think the idea of marriage is ridiculous."

"Perhaps it was."

"He's of the opinion that a certain Mark Gerson had a considerable influence over your sister-in-law. Do you know Mr Gerson?"

"I . . ." she began, then thought better of it. "No, Inspector, I don't—at least, not personally. I know of his shop in Moston, of course."

"Did Marcia ever talk of him to you?"

"Never."

"She did have an affair with him."

Helen Tucker did not answer, but again Mole noticed a tightening to the line of her mouth as though she were containing an explosive outburst.

He waited a moment, then said: "Did you know your sister-in-law was to have been married on the day she

116

was murdered?"

"How could I?" Her eyes softened, but still there was no shock, no suggestion of having been taken aback by the news. "That's awful," she said softly. "Did he—this solicitor—murder her?"

"I don't know, Mrs Tucker. There are still too many loose ends at the moment to be sure of anything."

"If he did, then he must have killed Charlie Stokes."

"Why?" asked Mole abruptly, his eyes narrowing.

"I don't know. It's just—well, it just seems logical somehow. Charlie must have known something, or seen something."

"Charlie Stokes seems to have seen and heard a lot," said Mole with a sigh.

"He was always nosing about," snapped Helen Tucker, now openly irritated. "Not that he could help it, I suppose."

"He didn't seem to get on well with your husband."

"No, that's true. They never had. He annoyed Alan, and Alan's not very good at hiding his annoyance. And I suppose you know Charlie was spreading a story about that Alan and Marcia were—having an affair?"

"Were they?" asked Mole flatly.

She smiled lightly at him as though forcing her face to physically register the stupidity of the suggestion. "Of course not."

"But they were closer than I was first led to believe?"

"Perhaps. It was only natural. We all rallied round in our own ways to comfort Marcia. Who wouldn't? But as for an *affair*—in that sense—it's silly!" She paused. "And in any case, Marcia had other fish to fry, it seems!"

Mole drummed his fingers on the steering wheel, aware of Helen Tucker's eyes on him, searching and waiting for a new reaction.

"Is your marriage a happy one, Mrs Tucker?" he asked suddenly, his fingers poised.

Helen Tucker caught her breath and started to flare,

her eyes growing wild, her hands clutching at the cardigan. Then she subsided almost as quickly, bringing herself into check with an icy smile.

"That is hardly worthy of you, Inspector. But I see the point of asking it. And the answer is—yes, perfectly happy, thank you. It always will be."

Mole felt the chill of her tone, started to speak but was dismissed instantly with a curt "Goodnight, Inspector!" and the slamming of the door in his face.

Helen Tucker walked quickly up the driveway to Blackstock without looking back. . .

"Ah—you're back, sir!" said Sergeant Fisher with a broad grin and a lengthening of his stride across the Operations Room at headquarters as he greeted Mole. "And I think we have our man!" he added with an extravagant wink.

Mole lifted one eyebrow in a long stare into Fisher's face as the Sergeant launched into an account of the "taking" of Steven Robins at Swinesleigh. "Not a bit of bother, sir," he concluded, "came as calm as a lamb. But he's worried, alright. Written all over him."

"Hmmm," said Mole when Fisher had finished. "Well done. Meanwhile, you've heard nothing of the possible sale of the Tucker farm, I suppose?"

"Sale, sir?" said Fisher, a frown knotting his eyebrows. "No, sir, nothing. Why, is it up for sale?"

"Alan Tucker reckons that Gerson had persuaded Mrs Tucker to sell and was acting on her behalf."

"Well, I've heard nothing, but I'll get someone on to it straightaway."

"Might be an idea," said Mole, reaching for a sheet of paper from a desk and hurriedly writing a name and number on it. "Tell Baxter to call this number and put them in the picture."

"Yes, sir," said Fisher, the frown disappearing and a glow returning to his face. "Oh, by the way, Mr Robins is in the interview room. Must be getting a bit impatient by now."

"We'll see," said Mole.

Fisher winked again at no one in particular, then followed Mole down the corridor and into the interview room. He dismissed the Constable and closed the door quietly behind him as Steven Robins came wearily to his feet.

## TWENTY-THREE

The steadiness of Steven Robins' stare into Mole's eyes lasted no more than seconds, but its intensity might have been an hour of burning appeal.

The man was scared. Mole could sense, almost reach out and touch the fear and doubt that had consumed him in the past few days. It showed in his lifeless flesh stretched like old paper over his bones; in the droop of his shoulders and the shaky fingers spreadeagled on the bare table-top. His clothes—a casual shirt and slacks—were rumpled and sweat-stained, and his feet shifted uneasily in slip-on canvas shoes.

For a man in his late thirties, professionally self-assured, rarely in doubt of his capabilities, almost unassailable, he looked now as if his years had doubled overnight to leave him bewildered and old in sudden defeat. The bewilderment of remorse, or the decay of guilt; the shape of a beaten man?

Not quite, thought Mole, as he apologised for having kept him waiting and motioned for him to sit down again. Mole settled with a sigh on the hard chair opposite, well aware that Robins' eyes were alive to his every movement; assessing, waiting.

"I . . ." began Robins, but his words collapsed in a croak. He tried again. "I'm the one who seems to have kept everyone waiting."

Mole missed none of Robins' struggle for confidence, the effort of coming to grips with himself which began almost instantly to show in his face—a well-bred face, thought Mole, with clean, easy angles. Not handsome, but uncluttered and sensitive.

"There has to be a very good reason for that, I'm sure," said Mole.

"Well . . ." said Robins, hesitating as Mole's gaze deepened on him.

Mole leaned back. "Shall we begin at the beginning, Mr Robins?" he said quietly. "From that first meeting with Marcia Tucker when Gerson introduced you to her. Or did it all begin in some other way at some other time?"

"It began then," said Robins, relaxing in his chair. His face was still ashen, but there was relief in his eyes and voice. "I knew, of course, that she was one of Gerson's women. But she was—well, different. I know that sounds shallow, but it's the only way I can describe her."

"Different in what way?" said Mole.

Robins thought for a moment, a clear line of new sweat breaking out on his top lip. "Well, once we started to see more of each other and to talk, it was obvious that all her brashness was an act. That wasn't the real Marcia at all."

Mole leaned forward. Robins' eyes clouded. He brushed the back of his hand quickly over the sweat line as though he knew what was coming.

"Before you go on, Mr Robins, were you planning to marry Mrs Tucker?"

Far away in the background, Sergeant Fisher cleared his throat and flicked to a clean sheet in his notebook.

"Yes, I was," said Robins.

Mole relaxed again. "It may seem an odd reaction on my part, but may I ask why?"

"Because we were in love, of course."

"Then may I also ask why you have been in hiding since last Friday and why you made no attempt to contact the police once it was known that the woman you were going to marry had been murdered? Hardly the actions of a man in love, Mr Robins!"

Robins flushed — the first hint of colour to cross his face for hours. But there was no anger. "That looks bad for me," he said softly.

"It looks," said Mole, "like the action of a man who was either very frightened — or very guilty."

"You think I murdered her?"

"I think you may have. Frankly, I don't have much alternative at the moment."

Robins tensed and sat forward, his hands flat on the table, his forehead saturated with sweat. "I didn't, you know! My god, I didn't!"

"Alright," said Mole, "let's assume that — for now. But let's go back — to last Friday in particular and your decision to leave Moston for the Saracen's Head. Why?"

"Marcia was to have met me there that evening. We were to have stayed the night and then gone on to London on Saturday and be married as soon as possible."

Mole tapped lightly on the table. "Mrs Tucker didn't arrive at the Saracen's Head on Friday night. Her body wasn't discovered until Monday. You made no attempt to find out why she hadn't turned up — or did you? Or did you just sit it out at Swinesleigh hoping that she'd arrive *sooner or later*, even though you must have known by early Tuesday that she was dead?" Mole's fingers fell silent. "Or perhaps you already knew she was dead? Perhaps you knew on Friday *after* you had

121

met her at the Cheal Crossing . . ."

"No!" snapped Robins, the colour deepening across his face. "I was at Swinesleigh all day Friday. I haven't left the place until this evening, I swear it!"

"Why?"

Mole's stare was steady and uncompromising. Robins looked anxiously from him to Fisher who had stopped writing, his pencil poised in his fingers like a spear.

"Because—because Marcia told me not to!"

"*Told you not to!*" Mole's voice pitched two octaves higher with incredulity.

"Yes, told me not to."

Mole sighed. "Alright, Mr Robins. When did she tell you—and for heaven's sake why?"

Robins dabbed fitfully at his forehead with a handkerchief, then screwed it into a tight ball in his clenched fist.

"There'd been a spot of trouble between us," he began, "and we'd decided to settle it on that Friday night. It was all—well, one of those idiotic situations that can happen to people in love."

He paused, dabbed again at his forehead, and continued: "Anyway, we arranged that I would go down to the Saracen's Head during Friday and she would join me that night. Then, at about mid-day, she telephoned to say that something concerning the farm had to be attended to and she wouldn't be able to make it that night—wouldn't be able to make it, in fact, until perhaps late Sunday or even Monday. I said straightaway that I'd leave and return to Moston and see her that night. No, she said, you mustn't do that. Stay where you are, she said, promise me. But why, I wanted to know, there was no point. I wasn't to worry, she said, everything would be alright but she needed at least the week-end to settle things once and for all. I asked her what she meant; what had happened to make her change her mind so suddenly. She hadn't changed her mind, she said, but what she had to attend to had to be done quickly and she thought it better if I were out of the way—out of Moston, out of Cheal End. She pleaded with me to stay at Swinesleigh, have a quiet week-end and look forward to either late Sunday or sometime Monday."

"And now you're asking me to believe that you did precisely that," said Mole flatly.

"Yes, Inspector, I am."

Mole stared deeply into Robins' eyes, waited a moment, then said: "You'd better carry on."

"After the call, I was so bewildered I hardly knew what to do. My first thought was to drive straight back to Cheal End and be with her. But she'd seemed so intense, so absolutely certain in her own mind that I wouldn't leave Swinesleigh, that I began to think perhaps it would be wiser to do as she said. You see, Inspector, Marcia and I had not had an easy time since our meeting. She had been playing it fairly fast and loose and we'd been forced to live in that shadow. There was Gerson, Henry Layton . . ."

"Not to mention Alan Tucker," interrupted Mole.

Robins flinched. "Yes—Tucker. That particular episode was at the root of our trouble."

"The rumoured affair. Was it true?"

"There had been something, I'm sure of that. And that had upset me more than anything. I could accept the others—but Tucker! The one man Marcia . . ." His voice trailed away and he shook his head. "It was Tucker we were going to discuss on the Friday night. Marcia knew how I felt, but she said she could explain and that I would understand." He paused.

"How did you come to hear of the affair with Alan Tucker?" asked Mole.

"Gossip to begin with. It had even reached Moston at one stage. At first, I didn't believe it, but it became an obsession with me. I had to know for certain, so I tackled the gossip at its source. I went to see Charlie Stokes."

Fisher coughed. Mole sighed.

"And I know that looks bad for me, too," said Robins.

"When did you see him?"

"On the Monday night before Marcia was murdered. I went to Cheal End—it was fairly late, about ten-o'clock, I think—and we met at the Fosbrick turn. Charlie told me what he knew, which was enough to make me want to discuss it with Marcia."

"What exactly did he tell you?"

"He told me he'd seen them together soon after Marcia's husband died at the time he was working for her. Apparently, Tucker would return to the farm in the evening and . . ."

"Did he actually *see* anything?"

"He said he'd seen Marcia in Tucker's arms. He'd seen them kissing and Tucker 'pawing' her, as he put it. Tucker eventually persuaded Marcia to sack Charlie."

"Did you believe him?"

Robins' eyes dropped and he took a deep breath. "I didn't want to, Inspector, but I had to have an explanation from Marcia. I thought both of us deserved at least that."

Mole slumped back in his chair and folded his arms. "Let's get back to the Saracen's Head."

"Well, after thinking about the call, I decided to stay. I had what I thought one very good reason for doing so," said Robins.

"Oh, and what was that?"

"Ever since our meeting, Marcia had been concerned for my career, my position as a solicitor. I know that may sound a little high-handed, but she had it firmly fixed in her mind that sooner or later my association with her would lead to trouble for me. Then, when we knew we were in love and going to marry, she worried about it even more. I told her not to be so foolish, that it didn't matter and that, in any case, once we were married we'd turn our backs on Moston. So, when I thought about the call, I guessed that whatever it was she had to arrange concerning the farm certainly didn't require my presence. I didn't agree with the way she thought about my position, but she did feel it deeply, and I had to respect it."

"So you stayed at Swinesleigh throughout Friday, Saturday, Sunday and Monday. What happened on Tuesday?"

Robins gave a slight shiver, dabbed at his forehead and top lip again, and buried the handkerchief back in his trouser pocket.

"I went quietly mad," he said slowly and in as level a tone as his welling emotion would allow. "I heard the news, and died with her." He paused. "At first, I rushed to my room, packed my bags and was about to head for the car when something—God alone knows what—stopped me. In a moment of vision, insight—I don't know—I suddenly realised that I would be a number one suspect. It was obvious that the police would very quickly discover the fact that Marcia and I were to be married. I owed Mark Gerson money—and he, more than anyone, would be on the prowl for his pound of flesh and ready to talk of what he knew and plenty of what he *thought* he knew. In a nutshell, Inspector, I panicked. I decided to stay at Swinesleigh. At least, I reasoned, while ever I was there I had the basis for an alibi for the Friday. There had to be someone in the pub who would vouch for my having been there. It didn't take long for me to realise that the whole of Marcia's past life would be dragged out and you would soon hear of her affairs with Layton and Tucker. It would be obvious, I thought, that I had a motive for murder—jealousy, hate, the wronged lover. Ridiculous, perhaps, but enough to finish me. I realise now, of course, I was wrong, selfish and stupid."

Robins' chin slumped to his chest. A few lank strands of his light-coloured hair were plastered into the sweat on his forehead; his hands, still and tense with the whites of the knuckles gleaming, crushed together in his lap.

Mole watched him in silence. When, he wondered, did love stop and self-preservation take over; where was the borderline, and how quickly could it be crossed?

"You say Mrs Tucker said she needed the week-end to settle things at the farm once and for all." Mole's voice was a steady drone across the room to which Robins reacted with a slow lifting of his head. "What did she mean?"

"I've no idea—no idea at all."

"Could it have concerned the sale of the farm?"

"The sale?" Robins' brow creased in puzzlement. "No, I don't think so. We'd often discussed it, of course, but agreed to leave the matter until we were married and settled in London."

"You had never heard of Mr Gerson showing any interest in the sale?"

"Gerson! Why should he? The farm had nothing to do with him."

"Quite so. But Mrs Tucker did say quite specifically that the matter delaying her joining you concerned the farm?"

"Specifically."

Mole was silent for a moment, his eyes half-closed in concentration. "What sort of relationship existed between Mrs Tucker and Gerson *after* he knew you were going to marry her?"

"He thought I was a fool to consider marriage. But, then, his idea of a relationship never got further than

126

the bedroom! However, he stopped seeing Marcia and left us alone. Well, almost. I owed him quite a lot of money—and so did Marcia—and that kept his interest in us very much alive!"

Mole came to his feet and walked over to the window that looked on to a courtyard at the back of headquarters. There was no one about and the night was still and very hot. He turned.

"Did you know that Henry Layton was being blackmailed as a result of his affair with Mrs Tucker?"

Robins spun round to face him. "Good heavens, no! By whom?"

"That we don't know," said Mole.

"I—I don't understand . . ." began Robins as he broke out in a fresh stream of sweat.

Mole walked back to the table. "Is there anyone—anyone at all—who might have known of your plans to meet at Swinesleigh on Friday? Now think very carefully, Mr Robins."

Robins waited, looking away from Mole to Fisher and then to the table-top. "I can't think of anyone. I certainly told no one—not even my Mother. She would have heard from me in London. And I'm sure Marcia wouldn't have mentioned it."

Mole nodded. "We'll have to check with the Saracen's Head as to your whereabouts on Friday—and where you were on the night of Charlie Stokes' death."

"Yes, of course. I'm sure there'll be someone . . ."

"In the meantime," began Mole, but was interrupted by the door opening and the appearance of a Constable who passed a note to Fisher.

"Excuse me, sir," said Fisher.

"Stay here, Constable." Mole followed Fisher out of the room and into the corridor.

"This has just come through, sir." Fisher held out the note to Mole. "There's been a fire at the Tucker

Farm!"

"What!"

"It's under control now, sir, but they've found a body in the kitchen."

Mole's face turned despairingly up into Fisher's.

"Whose?"

"Mark Gerson, sir. A very dead Mark Gerson."

# TWENTY-FOUR

Moston's Chief Fire Officer squelched through the mud and water like a black elephant taking a bath.

He reached the area of concrete where Mole, Fisher, a group of uniformed police and recuperating firemen stood watching the thick palls of smoke twist from the skeleton of what had once been the Tucker Farm, stamped his feet and coughed from deep within his stomach. "Bloody mess!" he wheezed and wiped a hand over his grime-covered face.

Mole grunted, thrusting his hands deeper into his pockets and letting his gaze wander over the scene.

The bungalow was no more than a blackened shell. Three of its four walls still stood like crunched and buckled cardboard, ghostly in the glare of vehicle headlights. The slate roof had collapsed to leave a grisly lattice-work of charred timbers scratched across the sky. Where once doors and windows had been closed to the outside world, now only pitiable gaps stared dead-eyed over Fenland. Grotesque tangles of furniture, clothing, pots, pans, cutlery, bedding, carpets were scattered across the yard in a water and mud-soaked jumble — the trimmings of life disintegrating in useless abandon. Mole noticed a pert white sling-back shoe still smouldering at the edge of a pool of water and watched it slowly melt to a pitted mass of bubbling plastic.

He looked away to where a group of villagers, huddled in coats and jackets flung hurriedly over nightwear, murmured and nodded among themselves, their eyes scanning the debris for the unusually horrific, the ridiculously distorted, the incredulously still recognisable. Fingers pointed, voices trembled, murmured and gasped in blank dismay and fascinated curiosity.

"Get that lot out of here!" he croaked to Fisher, who turned defiantly on the audience and splattered over the open ground towards them.

"We didn't stand a chance, Arthur," said the Fire Chief, wiping his face with a towel. "It'd been going fifteen minutes when we got here. God knows how we saved this much!"

"Where did you find the body?" asked Mole.

"Come on, I'll show you. It's safe enough now."

The Fire Chief squelched back into the morass, Mole following. He kicked aside a half-burned suitcase and slithered through a pulp of soddened ash.

"Round the back—or what's left of it," he called to Mole as they approached the gaping hole of the kitchen door.

"In here."

Mole's eyes smarted in the lingering smoke and a sheet of sticky sweat broke out on his back. He squinted into the heat-laden area trying to pinpoint something familiar—something, he reminded himself, which just over a day ago had been part of a home. He glanced round to the black webs of fitted cabinets, the crumpled shape of the table. His feet sloshed in water.

"He was there," said the Fire Chief, pointing to the area of floor beneath the twisted remains of the kitchen sink. "Face down. Another few minutes and he'd have been ash. Fortunately, one of my men made a bee-line for the kitchen in the event of there being bottled gas in storage. He broke in and—there he was. I recognised him straightaway."

Mole walked over to the spot. There was nothing to see. He scuffed his shoe-cap in the black mush. "How did it start?" he asked without looking up.

"Oh, not much doubt about that, Arthur! It was deliberate alright. Kerosene. Here, this way." He led Mole deeper into the smoking shell towards what was left of the Tucker's bedroom.

"Mind yourself, this lot's still smouldering. See, there." He pointed to an empty kerosene can lying on its side in a corner of the room. "Someone tipped that lot over the bed, we reckon, and set fire to it, then made a sharpish getaway out of the window."

"Obviously not Gerson," said Mole.

"Definitely not! From what I saw of the body before the ambulance arrived, he'd taken a real bashing on the side of the head. I reckon he was flat out before the fire started. Anyway, the Path boys'll confirm that."

Mole coughed and wiped the backs of his hands across his watering eyes.

"Mark you," said the Fire Chief, stamping his foot on a patch of smoking floor, "it's lucky that Alan Tucker chap over at Blackstock raised the alarm as fast as he did. A few more minutes and this lot'd have been a memory. Not that we saved much." He stamped at another patch of floor. "A pretty deliberate sort of job all round by the look of it. Murder and arson."

They made their way back to the kitchen and out into the yard.

"You've got your hands full with this lot, Arthur!" said the Fire Chief, unbuttoning his tunic.

Mole grunted, thanked him, and said he would appreciate having his report as soon as possible. Then he walked slowly away to where Fisher and Constable Lumby were in deep conversation by a patrol car.

Lumby stiffened to attention and settled his hat squarely on his head as Mole approached.

"Evenin'—I mean, mornin', sir," He passed a dry tongue into the dry corners of his mouth.

"Well?" said Mole. "What happened?"

"Like I was just telling Sergeant Fisher, sir. . . ."

"Tell the Inspector now!" said Fisher irritably.

"Like I was just telling Sergeant Fisher, sir . . ." round-the-clock watch on the place as you know, sir. The patrol car was due to go off at eleven, and I was here just as they were getting ready to go. I do a two-hour watch and then someone from Moston relieves me. I was putting my bike in the shed over there, then I heard this noise—a sort of scuffling in the barn. So I walked over and went in, but I couldn't see a thing. Must've been a rat or cat, I reckon. Anyway, when I came out again, there it was—the fire, I mean."

"You saw no one?" said Mole.

"Not a soul, sir."

"And?"

"Well, sir, I didn't waste time looking. I made straight for Blackstock—that being the nearest 'phone—and was just about to start shouting for someone when I saw Mr Tucker running from the house towards me. He'd called Moston and said the Brigade was on its way. We came back here, but there was nothing we could do. Couldn't get within yards of it, sir."

"Were there any windows open did you notice?"

"Windows, sir?"

"*Windows*, Lumby!" snapped Fisher.

"Well, not that I noticed, sir. I mean, I didn't really look, but there's been a back one on the latch since . . ."

"Alright, Lumby," said Mole. "You did your best. Put in a report immediately."

"Yes, sir."

"Go on, then, man!" said Fisher. "Get moving!"

Lumby trotted to his bike, mounted it, and wobbled away towards the village.

"Ye gods!" said Fisher, tugging at his shirt collar. "If this don't beat the lot! They tell me Gerson copped a bashing, sir?"

"Seems like it, Sergeant."

"What the devil was he doing here?"

"Three guesses," said Mole.

Fisher grunted. "The jewellery?"

Mole shrugged. "Maybe."

"*Inspector Mole!*"

Mole turned at the sound of his name to see Alan Tucker peering at him through the gloom. "Over here, Mr Tucker!" called Mole.

Tucker, his eyes streaming over ashen cheeks, his hair flattened with sweat, his shirt and trousers streaked with splashes of mud, hurried to join them.

"What a . . ." he began, shaking his head as he stared at the still smoking remains of the bungalow.

"We have to thank you for raising the alarm," said Mole.

"Yes—yes, I did what I could." Tucker turned to face him. "I saw the first sheet of flame from my study window. I was having a night-cap. Couldn't sleep after . . ." His voice petered out and he shivered. "It really is a nightmare, Inspector—a nightmare." His eyes moved across the devastation.

"Did you or Mrs Tucker see or hear anything, sir?" said Mole.

"No—no, nothing at all. Helen was in bed."

"Anyway, thank you for acting so quickly."

Tucker shivered again. "They say you found a body in there, Inspector."

"Yes, sir, unfortunately that is so. Mark Gerson."

Tucker's eyes closed. "My god!" was all he said, and turned to go.

"Someone will be along to see you later this morning, sir," said Mole to his back.

"Yes, of course . . ." he murmured as he walked across the yard to the road.

"Seems pretty shaken, sir," said Fisher.

"Aren't we all?" said Mole. "Still, there's nothing much we can do here. Get that kerosene can back to the lab. You never know, there might be a print left. And get some of the lads looking through what's left here for any signs of a weapon. Something heavy."

"Yes, sir."

"And you'd better have Baxter get round to Gerson's flat straightaway."

"I've done that, sir. Got through to him on a patrol car radio about twenty'minutes ago. He'll be there now, I shouldn't wonder. Oh, he sent a message to say he'd called that number you gave him and everything's fixed for you to see a Mr Cheek as soon as his office opens."

"Good."

"By the way, sir, Doctor Hill's here. Said she'd like a word if you have a minute. I'll see you later."

Fisher strode off to the group of Constables as Mole picked his way to the road where he found Jeanne Hill seated in her car.

"Am I in the way?" she asked.

"No," said Mole, "it's all over now. You'd best go home."

"I saw what was happening and thought I might be of some help."

"Thank you, but there's nothing you can do."

"Can I tempt you to a coffee? You look as if you could do with it."

"That's very kind, but I'm afraid it's back to

Moston, some sleep, some breakfast, and then work for me!"

"Of course, I understand." She paused. "I also wanted to apologise for running off like I did the other day. It was silly and . . ."

"There's no need," said Mole. "I think I know how you felt."

She stared ahead to where the dawn light crept slowly over the horizon. "Another hot day on its way," she said quietly.

"The last by the look of it," said Mole, screwing his eyes against the ache of sleep and smoke. "The rain's on its way. Anyway, I must be going. I'll take you up on that coffee later!"

She smiled and watched him walk away towards his parked car. Then, as she settled herself for the drive home, she shivered, but not because of her own lack of sleep or the chill of the deaths in Cheal End. It was simply that the dawn sky was already mellowing to thin streaks of grey-black cloud and a whisper of wind from the East was bending the grasses.

The Inspector had been right. The rains were coming.

## TWENTY-FIVE

Mole decided to forgo the sleep in favour of a breakfast of Evans' sausages and work — not an easy choice in the circumstances, but one that finally left him feeling surprisingly renewed as he made his way through Moston's Beck Alley to the offices of Cheek, Sims, Chubb & Sons, land agents and auctioneers.

He buttoned his jacket against the cooler East wind, glanced at the black rolling clouds overhead, then checked his watch. It was exactly eight-fifteen, and if he knew Bernard Cheek, the senior partner had been at his desk for at least twenty minutes. He was that sort of man—punctual, habitual, dedicated—which is why, thought Mole as he climbed the stairs in Berton Chambers to the first floor office, Cheek, Sims, Chubb & Sons had Fenland's respect for their integrity, fair dealing and no out of place favours, except on occasions. And this, for Mole, was one of them.

"Arthur! Good to see you," said Bernard Cheek, coming to his feet from behind a heavyweight walnut desk and dusting pipe ash from his tweed jacket.

"Good of you to see me at such short notice," said Mole, seating himself in the chair offered.

"Sergeant Baxter passed on the message—and I must say it came as a bit of a shaker. There's not been a whisper in these parts."

"It shook us," said Mole, relaxing.

"Anyway . . ." Cheek extracted a sheet of paper from a black folder, "I've had my hounds out and it looks as though you were right. Mark Gerson was trying to negotiate the sale of the Tucker farm. He was doing it through a Birmingham firm, Peal and Locke. I know them, vaguely, but we've had no dealings. Jack Sims—you know Jack, my partner?"

Mole nodded.

"Well, Jack's done a bit of business with them, so he started probing last night and finally managed to speak to Peal himself at his home. Seems that Gerson approached Peal about six weeks ago with the suggestion that a buyer be found for the farm. He said he was acting for the owner who would confirm the arrangement later, but nothing much happened after that. Peal started a tentative line-up of prospects but couldn't go too far, of course, until the owner gave a firm go-ahead. No figure had been mentioned at that time, by the way. Gerson told Peal to test the market—see what sort of price might be realised."

Cheek drew on his unlit meerschaum pipe, then put it aside. "After about a fortnight, Peal got in touch with Gerson and asked if the sale was definitely on and, if so, would the owner instruct accordingly." He looked up. "Peal thought he had a likely buyer at that time." His eyes went back to the sheet of paper. "Gerson told him there'd been a delay at his end and it might take a week or so before a definite go-ahead could be given. He gave no reason for the delay. Well, naturally enough, Peal dropped the matter at that point pending a final instruction."

"Hmmm," murmured Mole, stroking his chin and staring beyond Cheek to the window and the still gathering clouds.

"But that's not the end of it, Arthur. On the Thursday before her death, Peal received another call—this time from Mrs Tucker herself, who told him to forget any arrangements Gerson had made. The farm was definitely *not* for sale."

Mole sighed as Cheek folded the sheet of paper and handed it to him.

"Ah, well," said Mole, coming to his feet. "Thanks . . ."

"Sit down, Arthur!" ordered Cheek.

Mole slumped back in the chair.

"It doesn't end there." Bernard Cheek looked into the bowl of his pipe and fingered the loose ash reflectively. "It's not something I'd like this firm to be more generally known for," he began, "but there are times when—well, when I get interested, shall we say, and can bring a bit of influence to bear in the right quarters. Fact is, Arthur, I made a couple of 'phone calls myself last night after Jack had told me what he'd found out, and I think you should know that Alan Tucker was keeping very much up with the play over this prospective sale through his solicitors." He eyed Mole carefully. "Tucker knew of his sister-in-law's decision only hours after she made it. And from what I'm told—very confidentially, of course—he simply laughed!"

The sky had hardened to the steel-grey ceiling of the oncoming storm as Mole left Berton Chambers and walked quickly back to his office. He passed Mark Gerson's shop in Spillsgate, pausing only briefly to read the hand-written card propped in the window—"Closed Until Further Notice"—then hurried into the Square, turned right into Marsh Way and along the dockside towards headquarters. It was low tide and the fishing boats rode in a gentle half sleep as the freshening wind caught at the river's surface. A bevy of disgruntled gulls wheeled above the activities around a waterside warehouse, their calls drowned in the echoing clank of a loading crane's drive. Morning workers bustled by him, eyes scanning the sky in anxious anticipation of rain, fingers tugging at strangely unfamiliar raincoat collars. Mole crossed the road and took the steps to headquarters two at a time.

Fisher had slept for two hours, then washed, shaved and breakfasted in the canteen and was in deep conversation with Baxter when Mole called them into his office.

He went quickly through the details of his meeting with Bernard Cheek, then said: "Right, what's the news at this end?"

"I went round to Gerson's flat," said Baxter, "and found that woman, Ruby Lysaght, there. Apparently she and Gerson were together last night when he received a telephone call at about ten-thirty. She doesn't know who it was, but it put Gerson into a high old state of excitement, so much so that he said he'd have to go out for a while. He left soon after and said he'd be about an hour."

"The call that took him to the Tucker farm," said Mole.

"Seems like it, sir."

"And we think we've come up with the weapon used on Gerson, sir," said Fisher. "A hammer found in the rubble of the kitchen. There won't be any prints, but the lab reckons there'll be traces of blood. No such luck with the kerosene can, though—not a smudge of a print."

"Pity," said Mole.

"There's a lab report through on the black hairs found on the comb in Mrs Tucker's bedroom, but it's not a lot of help. Most likely a man's, is as far as they can go."

"Hmmm," murmured Mole.

"And if you want all the bad news together," added Baxter, "there's still nothing on Mrs Tucker's missing clothes, the weapon, or the blackmail letter. And we've done a thorough check on Alan Tucker's movements on the Friday, and they've been confirmed."

"Ah, well," said Mole with a sigh.

"Meanwhile," said Fisher, "Robins looks to have a watertight alibi for his days at Swinesleigh. The landlord of the pub reckons he was there all the time—never left—so I've let Robins go home as you instructed, sir."

"We'll need him later this morning," said Mole.

"Yes, sir, he understands that."

"What about Layton?"

"I've spoken to him, sir," said Baxter. "Says he was at home all last night, but he's agreed to your arrangements for later on."

Mole grunted.

"There is one other thing," began Fisher tentatively. "The Super would like a word with you."

"He can wait!" said Mole. "Now listen carefully both of you. This is what I want you to do . . ."

By eleven-o'clock on that November morning, it was generally agreed that the freak weather had passed, that it would be raining by noon and that a long, wet Winter would soon set in. Mole was prepared. He collected his raincoat and a pair of stout brogue shoes before driving out of Moston into the emptiness of Fenland.

The clouds, he noticed, were piled like old gravestones over Cheal End.

## TWENTY-SIX

Mole's legs were leaden and his body buffeted by the whip of the wind over open country as he made his way from the parked Hillman along the drive to the Tucker Farm. For all the certainty of his conclusions, he had no heart for their outcome. He would have been happy to have found himself walking in another direction, away from Cheal End and those he had come to meet. A quarter of a century of life in the Force had failed to harden him against the miseries of conviction, and he could sense even now the loneliness of those it would cross and leave in despair. And yet a murderer would be caught, justice seen to be done, and Fenland rid of an evil. Society would breathe again and he would move on to the next shadow. So much for the fictional triumph at the end of the trail! Death had no glory and murderers no glamour. And Police Inspectors, he reasoned with a quickening of pace, no time to reflect when there was a job to be done. . .

The smoke had cleared and the bungalow lay like a black carcass at the edge of the yard, an unremitting epitaph, thought Mole, to the struggle that had been the lot of John and Marcia Tucker. He walked on, his eyes fixed on the barn and the silent figures that stood waiting for him at its open doors. Faces turned as he drew nearer — Henry Layton, Steven Robins, Alan Tucker, Helen Tucker, Sergeant Fisher — but remained impassive and, in all but one instance, uncomprehending.

Five pairs of anxious eyes tracked Mole's steps into the barn and watched his face as he murmured an almost inaudible good morning. He paused, waiting for Alan Tucker — as he knew he would — to be the first to speak.

"There's a storm brewing," said Tucker, hunching himself into his padded parka. "Wouldn't we be more comfortable indoors? Blackstock is at your disposal, Inspector."

Henry Layton grunted his approval, then turning to Mole, said: "Is it really necessary to be out here? And why, in heaven's name, are we here?"

Mole glanced round the group. They were an assorted bunch, he mused. Alan Tucker in his constructed executive neatness beneath his off-hand coat; Henry Layton, looking as though he had found a good dog sick at the start of a day's shooting; Helen Tucker, classic and delicate as ever in tweed skirt, polo neck sweater and incongruously "sensible" shoes, and Steven Robins, who had nicked his chin in a hurried shave and fingered the paper plaster nervously when his hands were not rummaging absent-mindedly in his raincoat pockets.

Mole cleared his throat. "I'm sorry about the weather, but as for being here, I think you all know the reason for that. We are here because of three murders. This is where it all began and this, I think, is where it should end."

"Sensitively put, Inspector," said Tucker with a barely discernible sneer, "but hardly practical in . . ."

"You know who killed Marcia," said Robins hoarsely.

The others turned to stare at him and then, silently, at Mole.

"I believe I know *why* she was murdered, Mr Robins," said Mole. "And I've been searching for an answer to that since Charlie Stokes found her body."

Mole paused. No one spoke. Their eyes remained fixed on his face.

"I have never regarded her murder as having been committed in outrage or uncontrollable hate," he went on. "It was planned and executed with considerable care."

"Are you trying to tell us, Inspector," said Tucker, "that my sister-in-law wasn't murdered in a moment of—shall we say, high emotion—by one of her frustrated or even rejected lovers?"

"If you . . ." began Robins angrily.

"Oh, I don't expect *you* to go along with that!" snapped Tucker. "But the fact is that she was half undressed when Charlie found her. If you can't see . . ."

"Alan!" shouted his wife.

Robins took a step forward, only to find his path to Tucker barred by the bulk of Fisher.

"On the face of it," said Mole, "I have to agree that it certainly looked that way, Mr Tucker. With one exception."

"And what was that?" asked Layton.

"The clothes. They were missing. In fact, they still are. Now, I think I may claim a little more experience of these matters than any of you, and I can assure you that had Marcia Tucker been murdered in, as you put it, Mr Tucker, a moment of high emotion, frustration or even rejection, the last thing her killer would have concerned himself with is the confiscation of her clothes."

"This is awful!" Helen Tucker shuddered.

"I'm sorry, Mrs Tucker," said Mole, "but it's important to understand this part of the situation, because having accepted that the murder had no definite sexual motive, then we must assume that Marcia's murderer went to some lengths to ensure that we would be led to that conclusion—when, in fact, she was murdered for quite another reason."

"Circumstantial, Inspector," said Tucker. "Her reputation more than offsets any such assumption. You know what she was."

Again Robins fumed, and this time Fisher laid a gentle but determined arm across his chest.

"Do I, Mr Tucker? I know what my officers have discovered of her activities and what each of you has told me."

"I, for one, was never convinced that she was all that bad," said Layton. "I never saw that side of her—never."

"Well, I did!" scoffed Tucker, his eyes shooting to Robins' face.

"I believe that," said Mole. "I believe that you, Mr Tucker, were the first to take advantage of her vulnerable position."

"*Vulnerable position*! What the devil's that supposed to mean?"

"Alan!" Helen Tucker's eyes flashed to her husband's. Then, as the others watched her, she said more gently: "Let him finish, please."

Mole waited.

"Well, Inspector?" said Tucker.

"Let's go back to the death of your brother," began Mole. "His death may or may not have caused you some grief—that is unimportant. What is important is the prospect it opened up for you of adding to Blackstock's wealth. Your problem lay in how best to set about achieving it, bearing in mind your sister-in-law's resolve to farm the land herself. So, I believe, you tried a tactic at which you have a deal of proficiency. You tried charming her into selling. First, no doubt, by a carefully calculated measure of sympathy and understanding, and then as your association deepened, through a more physical and intimate approach. You tried to have an affair with her."

Tucker's lips tightened, but he remained silent.

"And," said Mole, "you almost succeeded. Certainly, you were making considerable headway by the time Charlie Stokes became suspicious of your night time visits. But at some point, you overplayed your hand. Marcia came to realise that your affection and apparent commitment to her were really no more than a cover for your ambitions to own the land. That was the breaking point for her — and she began her new life, the one for which she was to earn the reputation of whore. You created that, Mr Tucker."

"Not a shred of evidence to prove a word of it," croaked Tucker.

"None is necessary — for the moment," said Mole, pausing to glance at the others. "And so," he went on, "Marcia Tucker took to her new life with some relish, but she soon found herself spending far too much money, particularly with Mark Gerson to whom she became over-committed. It may well have seemed to her at that time that life had finally deserted her — until you, Mr Robins, came on the scene. That changed everything. Marcia found love."

Robins passed a hand across his forehead, then looked away through the open barn doors, across the dull fields to the storm clouds.

"The damage, however, had been done," said Mole. "Mark Gerson was soon pressing for a sale of the farm in an attempt to not only retrieve whatever Marcia owed him, but true to form, to extract a little more — a lot more, in fact. You, on the other hand, Mr Tucker, were making no progress at all. Gerson never discussed with you the prospects of Marcia's marriage, of course, because he knew that if the news became general knowledge, then his own influence would slip out of sight. But he did tell you of the plan he had for the sale of the farm, a taunt which he could not resist and which, I have no doubt, he considered might well push up the price, for if he were to maintain control of the sale it was very likely that he would reap the full benefit of any counter bid made by yourself. By telling me of Gerson's plan, you hoped I would automatically assume that Marcia had in some way frustrated it, giving Gerson good reason to kill her.

"It was news of Gerson's move, however, that clinched the situation for you, particularly when you were also told by your solicitors on the Thursday before Marcia's death that she had contacted the Birmingham agents chosen by Gerson and instructed them that the farm was definitely not for sale. What you did not know was that Marcia had already decided to *sell to you* following the call you made to her to arrange a meeting for Friday — which I shall come to in a moment.

"However, to you it appeared that you had every reason to go ahead with your plan to murder your sister-in-law, thus leaving the land in other hands — almost certainly her brothers in Canada — who, as likely as not, would be only too pleased to negotiate a quick sale. And with Marica out of the way, Gerson's power would collapse."

Tucker straightened, thrusting his hands deep into the pockets of his parka. "Fascinating!" was all he said.

"Your plan," continued Mole, "was straightforward enough. You had, as I say, telephoned your sister-in-law on Thursday and made an arrangement to meet her on Friday. She, perhaps reluctantly at first, agreed to the meeting knowing full well what you wanted to discuss. But on the other hand, a sale to you might be just the answer she was looking for. Suppose, she thought, she did sell to you? That would certainly leave Gerson high and dry, and there was no reason now, with her marriage plans well ahead, why she shouldn't sell. After all, she and Robins had no intention of living in Fenland, anyway. Unfortunately, she did not communicate this to you over the telephone. Had she done so, she would not have died. Instead, she contacted the Birmingham agents cancelling the arrangement made by Gerson. She also telephoned Mr Robins to warn him that there would be a delay to their proposed week-end together. Again, unfortunely, she left this call until the Friday morning, because it was not until then, I believe, that she had come to a final decision to sell to you. There was also another reason for the delay: she wanted Mr Robins safely out of the way before completing any such sale — to you, of all people! As she reasoned to herself and pointed out to Mr Robins, all would be satisfactorily explained very soon. Quite right, it would have been.

"And so, on that Friday afternoon, Mr Tucker, you made your way from Moston to Cheal End, having gone to some pains to create an apparently watertight alibi for your movements. Your intention was to meet Marcia, kill her, and quite simply return home to Blackstock. Marcia had insisted on the meeting at Cheal End at the farm where, I also believe, she would have accused you of having sent a blackmail letter to Henry Layton. She believed you had sent it as part of your revenge for the stories Charlie Stokes was putting about, and it may have been of some, shall we say, beneficial influence to her in the negotiations for the sale. You, of course, would have preferred the meeting elsewhere, but no matter, you felt you could cope with the situation.

"All very neat, swift and sure. By that Friday night, you would be the new owner of the Tucker land, or at least as close to ownership as made little difference.

"But something went wrong. When you reached the farm, Marcia was not to be found—because by then, of course, she was already lying dead in the dyke at the Cheal Crossing."

## TWENTY-SEVEN

A long, low peal of thunder rumbled in from the East to bring the first fall of rain to Fenland for a month, but to those gathered in the barn it arrived unnoticed.

Alan Tucker, his face suddenly lean and pale, stared at Mole as though confronting an apparition. Layton and Robins were silent and still, their mouths dry, their eyes unblinking. Helen Tucker's hand slid from her husband's arm to hang loosely at her side. Fisher thrust his hands behind his back.

Mole walked to the open doors, lifted his face to the sky and without looking at the group, said: "No, Mr Tucker, you did not murder your sister-in-law. You were too late. Someone had beaten you to it."

He turned sharply, his eyes keen and bright but slow moving over the faces of his audience. "Who was that someone?"

Another clap of thunder grumbled among the clouds, this time directly overhead. The rain fell faster as the wind died and the air chilled in the downpour.

"It could not have been Mark Gerson," said Mole. "He had everything to lose by Marcia's death, and on the Friday in question he kept an appointment in Moston until at least five-thirty. It could not have been Mr Robins, because he was at Swinesleigh. Mr Layton was at his home until four-o'clock, but could, given a fast car and clear roads, have reached Cheal End in time for a meeting with Marcia."

Layton's mouth opened but he made no sound.

"On the other hand, Mr Layton had already had the perfect opportunity to murder Marcia Tucker when he visited the farm and confronted her with a blackmail letter. Did he choose to miss it in favour of a more detailed plan to be put into operation on Friday?"

"That's not true!" spluttered Layton. "I was . . ."

"But why would he have chosen to meet her at the Cheal Crossing? Why not at the farm?" said Mole, disregarding Layton. "The only explanation of that, as I see it, is that whoever met Marcia at the Crossing did so because he already knew that Alan Tucker had arranged to meet her at the farm and could not risk the chance of his arriving there at the wrong moment — or, perhaps more important, did not want him implicated. Is that not so, Mrs Tucker?"

Helen Tucker came to a physical full-stop. There was no movement — not a breath that escaped her, not a muscle that moved in her suddenly tensed body. Her mouth was a closed, tight line, her eyes as steady on Mole's face as the glare of unshaded lights. The others turned to look at her — Robins, with an expression of loss and incredulity; Layton, bewildered and his breathing fast and nasal; Alan Tucker, mouth open, eyes glazed, his paleness draining still further into sickly grey. He made an attempt to speak, but the words were smothered in a groan.

"It took you a long time to plan the events of that Friday, Mrs Tucker, but you were thorough and very nearly — so very nearly — successful."

"You'll have to do better than that, Inspector!" she

said, her voice sharp and incisive, her eyes flashing the defiance Mole had seen on the night of their last meeting.

"I will," said Mole. "I will tell you precisely what happened on that day."

"For God's sake, Inspector!" snapped Tucker.

"One moment, Mr Tucker. Let's go back to your attempts to persuade your sister-in-law to sell the farm."

"Alright! Alright!" said Tucker hysterically. "I admit what you say! I did try to have an affair with Marcia! I did plan to . . ."

"Keep your mouth shut!" snarled his wife.

They stared at each other, the silence between them as heavy as the thunder that continued to roll in from the East.

"Your wife, of course, knew from the very beginning the tactics you were employing to buy the farm," said Mole, walking deeper into the barn. "She had seen them many times before, I believe; times when you flirted so easily with a new face, when a woman could not be resisted in pursuit of either fresh pleasures or business deals, and sometimes both. It was nothing new and perhaps a situation she had come to accept — until it moved in next door.

"You wanted your husband to own the land," said Mole, turning to Helen Tucker. "You wanted it almost as desperately as he did, but for a different reason. You believed that it might settle him once and for all; give him a new incentive in business by fulfilling his ambition of seeing all Tucker land under the ownership of Blackstock. But the asking price became too high.

"You could see no relief from the anguish of having Marcia so close — there for your husband to make up to whenever he thought there might be a chance she would sell. So, like him, you decided on what seemed

148

the only course open to you—remove Marcia from the scene. Your plan, of course, was much more elaborate. You decided from the very outset to use Marcia's reputation as your means of throwing suspicion on what could be any one of a string of men. You planned a murder with a very obvious sexual motive. As it happened, a shade too obvious!"

Mole paused, glanced round the faces of the group, then continued: "Your first move was to aquaint yourself fully with the reputation Marcia was earning. And that wasn't difficult. You had only to keep your ears open to discover those closely associated with her. Charlie Stokes, who had a deal of affection for you, I suspect, was not slow to add as much as he knew—including the details of your husband's affair with Marcia. However, it was Henry Layton you chose as the first pawn in your plan. He was to receive your blackmail letter. It was a safe bet that Layton would contact Marcia and thus begin the state of confusion you planned. He, you reasoned, would become the first suspect.

"As to the murder itself—you knew exactly how you would go about that, but the date, at that time, had not been fixed. And then two things happened to make you select Friday.

"Firstly, in a moment of her own excitement at the prospect of marriage, Marcia told you of her intentions when you met in the store in Moston. That must have thrown you slightly until you realised that a marriage, while perhaps removing some of the dangers of a continuation of the affair with your husband, would also make it certain that the land would never become a part of Blackstock. Worse, it might mean that Marcia and her husband would return to live at the farm! Time, nevertheless, was still on your side, although you did not know of Marcia's arrangements to go to Swinesleigh. All you could assume was that the wedding would not be too distant. Later, you were to put the marriage prospect to good use by being the first to tell me of it and begin the hunt for the husband-to-be who, of course, was sure to become the number one suspect.

"Then, I believe, you came to hear of the meeting your husband planned with Marcia. He certainly did not mention it to you, but it's my guess that you overheard his telephone conversation making the arrangement. And that convinced you that you had to act quickly. You feared a revival of the affair, and it now seemed obvious that your husband, far from having lost interest in Marcia, was cultivating the relationship. So you made your arrangement to meet her.

"The weather was pleasant — what about a meeting at the Crossing? True, it was in the open, but if you chose your time carefully — late afternoon — you might just succeed in being alone with Marcia long enough for what you had in mind. The meeting could certainly not be at the farm because you knew that your husband would arrive there later that afternoon. And so you met Marcia — she no doubt willingly agreeing in the belief that your interest in her marriage was genuine — and killed her with a knife taken from your own kitchen. You then removed her underclothing to give the impression of a sexual murder — and sat back content in the knowledge that it would be obvious that Marcia had been murdered by one of her so-called lovers.

"But you had overlooked entirely the threat presented by Charlie Stokes. He turned out to be not quite so simple. He knew of your concern over the affair between your husband and Marcia and soon realised that you, Mrs Tucker, had been the only person in Cheal End to take any real notice of his stories — and what's more, believe them. That, so far as

Charlie was concerned, put you at the top of his list of those with a hate big enough to murder for. Did Charlie talk to you of his suspicions, or did he try to blackmail you? Whatever, you knew he would eventually tell someone—most probably me—that you had been questioning him about Marcia's activities. He was also too precise in his accounts of what he had seen at the Tucker farm—and that meant your husband would come under suspicion.

"Your plan to murder Charlie followed a similar pattern. You arranged a late night meeting with him, no doubt to discuss either his blackmail threat or by tempting him in some other way—not difficult in view of his regard for you. In Charlie's case, of course, the actual killing would need a deal more strength if it was to be done with the same weapon. And that was vital if you were to maintain the impression of the murders having been committed by a man. However, once seated in your car, it would not have been difficult to move close to him and with one quick lunge . . ."

A sheet of lightning lit up the sky.

"You took a considerable risk in dumping the body in the dyke, but it was necessary to continue what you now saw as a definite pattern. You were not seen and, once again, you could afford to relax. The danger to both yourself and your husband had been eliminated.

"The Police would undoubtedly come to hear of the stories Charlie had been putting about, but with both Charlie and Marcia dead, the coast, as they say, seemed clear. Clear, that is, until your husband told you of my visit to Blackstock on the night I gave you a lift, and for the first time confided in you the fact that Mark Gerson had been endeavouring to sell the farm on Marcia's behalf. At first this did not concern you until you quite suddenly realised that Gerson could pose yet another threat. Sooner or later, I would have investigated his plans for the sale which would again

151

shift the emphasis of suspicion on to your husband. But now time was really against you. Then you conceived the plan of bringing Mark Gerson to Cheal End that very night on the pretext of retrieving Marcia's jewellery from the farm.

"But you could not afford to be away from Blackstock for more than, say, thirty minutes at the outside. You made the contact with Gerson and, with your husband consoling himself with a few Scotches in his study, slipped out to the Tucker farm, entered by the window at the kitchen — fortunately for you left on the latch — and awaited Gerson's arrival.

"You had warned him, of course, of the patrol car, but he had no difficulty in arriving unseen. You knew that you had no hope of killing Gerson in the same way you had Marcia and Charlie. This had to be a quick and sure job. One sound and . . . But again, you had timed things well. The patrol car would leave and Lumby take over — that had been the routine for the past few days, which you had doubtless observed from Blackstock. You had told Gerson to enter by the back door, which would be open to him, and come into the kitchen where you, of course, would be waiting. Your blow to his head with the hammer was decisive enough. But you had no time to be absolutely certain that he was dead, so you created a diversion which would also serve as a guarantee that Gerson died. You set fire to the bungalow. True, the fire may prove a hindrance to you in getting away, but it would also act as the complete cover for your re-entry to Blackstock. Lumby would obviously head for the farm for help, your husband would assist and then go with him to the fire — and you would return unnoticed."

Mole paused.

"Your only mistake, Mrs Tucker, was your decision to murder Marcia at the Cheal Crossing. That location, for all the reputation your sister-in-law had of being free and easy, was out of character. She would never have agreed, in my opinion, to a meeting there for that purpose. But you have your husband to thank for forcing that decision on you. And you should have left her clothing behind. You made a poor team in marriage, it seems, and a non-existent one in murder."

The rain reached a crescendo, a ceaseless downpour that set the yard awash, turned the ploughed fields to a dark brown mass beneath the grey of the sky and shattered the silence that followed.

Helen Tucker remained perfectly still, unaware of those about her. Slowly, deliberately, her husband's hand went out to her, reached her arm but could not grip. She smiled at Mole, brushed Alan Tucker's hand aside and walked out of the barn into the torrent of rain.

Fisher made a move to stop her, but was checked by Mole. "No, not yet," he said quietly.

She reached the edge of the yard, paused and looked back, the rain streaming from her hair to her face, her clothes soddened and lifeless over her slim figure.

"Damn Blackstock!" she screamed.

"Helen!" The word sprang from Alan Tucker's throat in a splintered cry as he reached the yard, then halted, arms limp at his sides. His wife laughed in his face, turned and walked away.

Baxter and three Constables climbed from their parked cars and moved towards her from the road, but there was no hesitation in her steps as she neared them.

Two minutes later she was seated in the back of the leading car as the convoy headed for Moston.

Alan Tucker shuffled, head down, into the barn. He looked at Mole but said nothing. Only his eyes, in their pale, sad blueness, revealed the despair he could not voice.

## TWENTY-EIGHT

Mole had never eaten so well or with such relish. He could not recall a meal like it; certainly, he had never seen such a dish served, let alone been the guest of its creator. It had been sheer artistry, a talent given full rein to go its way in search of perfection — and then, as far as he was concerned, achieve it. Would that such experiences were the everyday lot of the policeman!

He sat back, lifted the brandy glass, and looked appreciatively across at Jeanne Hill. "That," he pronounced, "was superb!"

She smiled. "Why, thank you kind sir!"

"I mean it. I haven't eaten like that in — in a lifetime!"

She tilted her head in acknowledgment. "I think you needed it."

"Yes, I think you're right." Mole's eyes went beyond her to the windows, the night and the unseen shapes of Cheal End. "A fortnight ago, I sat in this very room . . ." His voice drifted away. "Ah well, it's all over now."

Jeanne Hill was silent for a moment, then said: "What will happen to her?"

"Helen Tucker? Oh, there'll be an interminable round of psychiatric reports, then the trial, and eventually, I suppose, a life sentence. I doubt if she'll plead insanity. She's not the type."

"Was she, is she — insane, I mean?"

"No, not in my book. Quite the opposite, in fact. A more level-headed person would be difficult to find.

No, she knew what she was doing, and how it had to be done. It's my guess she'll plead guilty. Her counsel has already advised it. But had it not been for the missing clothes — which, incidentally, we've recovered along with the weapon from Blackstock — and the change of location, well . . ."

"It's the deliberate way she went about it I find so hard to understand. I somehow can't believe she'd do all those terrible things."

"Physically, or mentally?"

"I'm not sure . . ."

"It's a common enough mistake to assume that a murderer has to be someone built for the job, when in fact you have to look for a person capable mentally of conceiving the plan. The execution is a case of mind over matter. A sound plan produces all the strength necessary."

"And yet the irony of it is that Marcia would have died on that Friday, anyway."

"Quite," said Mole. "If Alan Tucker had had his way, there's a good chance she'd have been dead by six-o'clock. But if Marcia had told him of her intention to sell the farm to him, he would have cancelled his plan — and that, of course, would have meant that Helen would have abandoned hers. If Marcia had told Robins of her decision, that would have saved her, because he would have left Swinesleigh and joined her. As it was . . . well, Helen Tucker was protecting her marriage. Marcia was protecting her husband-to-be. Robins was protecting himself and Marcia against the past. Protection became a confusion that led to elimination. And that protective instinct was bred in fear of the future. Helen, Alan, Marcia, Robins — they all doubted their futures. At the same time, they all believed they could shape their destinies by their own deeds. It didn't work."

"What about Alan Tucker?"

"He's already decided to sell Blackstock and travel overseas. He has little choice. Cheal End holds nothing for him now."

"So Blackstock changes hands after all these years?"

"Yes, as will the Tucker farm. Marcia's relatives in Canada have decided to sell."

"And poor Steven Robins?"

"He says he'll take up an appointment in London. In his case, it's the wisest and most sensible move. He'll recover, but never forget. There's a long life ahead of him, but it could never be lived in Fenland."

"And meanwhile, I suppose Henry Layton . . ."

"Henry Layton has returned to Cromford and his wife, which is where he always belonged."

"And Inspector Mole — what of him?"

Mole smiled. He rummaged in his jacket pocket, found the thimble he had picked up under the bridge at the Crossing, and placed it on the table.

"I've no idea who this belongs to," he said, "but after I discovered it in the dyke where Marcia was found, I carried it with me in the fond hope that it might be a clue. It wasn't. But Sergeant Fisher asked early on how many men went about with a thimble in their pocket. Not many, I suppose. That thought didn't really have any significance until Mark Gerson died. And then I thought: well, if it didn't belong to a man, then it must have belonged to a woman."

"But it's not Helen Tucker's?"

"Oh, no — not at all. As Fisher suggested, it was probably dropped by a child, or taken by a Magpie. But it made me think of a woman! So when you ask what of me — well, I am tempted to say that a thimble gave me the inspiration to think that the murderer might be a woman!"

"I don't believe you!"

Mole smiled again. "You'll never know, will you! But talking of inspiration — that inspires me to wonder if,

156

when Superintendent Hayes and the Chief Constable have finished grilling me over this case, you would accept an invitation to dine one evening at Bird Dyke? I can't promise a setting as tasteful as this, or a dish to compare with the one you've just served. But I make a fair job of sausages!"

It was late when Mole left Cheal End and drove through the village towards the Crossing and the road to Moston. The steady rain of the past week had eased to showers, but now the land was fresh and vital and already the once skeletal grasses had begun to lift in a rush to new life. As he crossed the bridge at the Crossing, he paused just long enough to catch sight of the fast flow of water along the dyke—washing away forever the dust and death of that freak November.